"I'd never get tired of looking you. Never."

Harley hooked her fingers in the sides of her garter belt, wanting to put her hands somewhere preferably on Grant, yet he remained a foot away, circling her.

"I wouldn't mind something interesting to look at," she challenged.

"All you had to do was ask."

One tug divested him of his bow tie. Ditto for the belt. Like a stalking cougar, he continued to circle her, popping one button, then another, until she could see the dark hair curling on his toned chest. Her breath abandoned her. Her breasts tingled.

He unhooked his pants, leaving them lazily open on his hips. "I do believe I'm stripping for you. How'm I doing?"

"If you want my professional opinion, I don't remember. But *I'd* definitely pay money to watch you undress."

"Sorry, I don't take cash."

Harley turned to him, breathless as he shed the last of his clothes. "Credit cards? Checks?"

He shook his head and took her hands. *"Nothing but trade, darling, nothing but trade."*

Dear Reader,

When I think BLAZE, I think fantasy. Push-the-limits
fantasy. Cross-the-line fantasy. Fantasies that make you
blush, even when you're alone.

My favorite kind.

My first BLAZE, *Seducing Sullivan,* featured characters
with unresolved desires from the past—characters destined
to reunite. For my second BLAZE, I wanted something
different. I wanted to bring together a man and a woman
who didn't have any business even being in the same
room, much less the same bed. A man and a woman so
drawn to each other, they're willing to gamble everything
in exchange for the briefest moment of ecstasy.

Once Harley and Grant meet, however, the ecstasy is
anything but brief. Harley's a woman with a secret—a
scandal waiting to happen. Grant can't afford even a hint
of gossip thrown in his direction, and yet Harley proves
too tempting to resist.

The risks heighten. The tension soars. Ooh, I love writing
for Temptation!

Grant and Harley teach each other quite a bit about the
price *and* the rewards of true, uninhibited passion—a
desirable lesson to learn. I hope *Private Lessons* heats up
your day—and your nights. After all, that's what BLAZE
is all about.

Sincerely,

Julie Elizabeth Leto

P.S. I'd love to hear from my readers. Please write to:
P.O. Box 270885, Tampa, FL 33688-0885.

PRIVATE LESSONS
Julie Elizabeth Leto

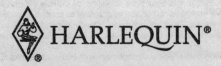

HARLEQUIN®

TORONTO • NEW YORK • LONDON
AMSTERDAM • PARIS • SYDNEY • HAMBURG
STOCKHOLM • ATHENS • TOKYO • MILAN • MADRID
PRAGUE • WARSAW • BUDAPEST • AUCKLAND

For Joy Leto and Sue Kearney—who read every word
with a critical eye, who offer unending support and
encouragement, who listen and comment and collaborate
as only best friends can.
And for Brenda Chin, whose editorial talent is eclipsed
only by her ability to cultivate and coax the best from her
authors. Thanks for not letting me be a
"one-book wonder."

ISBN 0-373-25824-0

PRIVATE LESSONS

Copyright © 1999 by Julie Leto Klapka.

1

"HEY, LADY, YOU dishin' out more than fifty bucks, or what?"

The cabdriver's question snapped Hailey Roberts's thoughts away from the imposing mansion behind the gate. Her chest constricted at the mention of money. Once she parted with the crumpled Ben Franklin in her pocket, she wouldn't have a penny to her name. Until the end of the evening. When she got paid for taking off her clothes.

Her stomach roiled.

"Fifty is all I have. You said it would be enough."

Why was he in such a hurry? She glanced from her watch to the rotating meter. She still had ten dollars and eighty...no, seventy...cents' worth of time to muster the courage she needed to leave the cab. Suddenly sweltering in her sturdy trench coat, she scooted nearer the open window, but found no relief from the sultry Florida heat.

Even so, she shivered.

"How 'bout leavin' some of your dough for a tip, huh?" the cabby begged. "This wasn't no quick drive downtown. It'll take me half an hour to get back to the strip."

As her body temperature rose, Hailey's heart thudded against her ribs, sending pulses of pain straight to the back of her eyelids. She hated causing trouble, even for grumpy, New-York-transplanted cabdrivers trying to rush her into the most humiliating situation she'd ever faced. Not that she was a stranger to humiliation. She'd spent the better part of her life swallowing her pride and delaying her dreams. Aunt Gracie needed constant proof that Hailey and her baby brother, Sammy—only one year old when their parents died—were more than just cramps in her life-style and extra mouths to feed. Hailey'd finally found the courage to break away and start a better life for herself and Sammy. No matter what the cost.

It's now or never, Hailey, love. You've got tonight or the streets. Then where will Sammy be?

Her grim predicament fueled her ire. Who did this guy think he was, making her feel guilty just because she wasn't eager to rush her degradation? Hadn't Aunt Gracie used similar tactics over the past fifteen years to ensure Hailey's adherence to her rules? Hailey grabbed the back of the driver's seat like a lifeline. "You want a tip, lose the meter."

Oh, Lord. Hailey snapped her mouth closed with an audible pop, horrified by how much she'd sounded, at that moment, exactly like the aunt she wanted so desperately to escape. Constant exposure to the woman's verbal spite manifested into sharp words whenever Hailey found herself backed into a corner. She'd come out swinging before she could stop herself.

Hailey pushed Gracie's voice out of her head and found her own. "If I had more than fifty, I swear, I'd give you a great tip for making the long drive. But I'm broke. Please, I just need another minute, okay?"

The cabby, blessed with a baby face and kind eyes to offset his coarse voice, shoved his cap back on his forehead. He readjusted the rearview mirror to watch her more closely, then sighed and flipped off the meter.

"Two minutes. Not three. I gotta living to earn and I

ain't gonna pick up no fares in a swank neighborhood like this."

She exhaled, though the reflex failed to relax her. "Two minutes. Thank you."

Peering out the rear window, she nodded in agreement with the cabdriver's assessment of Wellesley Manor. The subdivision in Citrus Hill, Florida, definitely rated as "swank", if not "posh" and "exclusive" as well. The homes, constructed of brick in myriad shades from red to amber and designed with more columns than the Coliseum, sat back from the roadways on well-tended, tree-draped lawns. She'd trek quite a distance to the front door of 724 Wellesley Lane, the address her cousin had scribbled on the napkin now clutched in her palm.

Perspiration muted the ink, but Hailey could still read the address well enough to compare it to the gleaming brass numbers on the gate. She'd always wanted to see the inside of a mansion in an exclusive neighborhood like Citrus Hill.

But like this?

Cradling her head in her hands, she inhaled deeply, mindless of the stale stench permeating the cab's floor. With any luck, the resident of 724 Wellesley Lane didn't routinely hire strippers. A regular would spot her inexperience in a flash. Mary Jo might believe Hailey would be a natural, but Hailey couldn't fathom how she'd reached such a dire situation in so short a time.

How could she possibly disrobe in front of strange men?

Her cousin had tried to reassure her. "You're a professional dancer. You take your clothes off in dressing rooms all the time," Mary Jo rationalized. "Half the costumes you wear don't amount to much more than a bikini. Besides, this guy's nice. He's really not as raunchy as he likes everyone to think. The whole thing's just a joke on his uptight brother, anyway. Hailey, love, you can do this. You have to unless you want my mother raising Sammy without you around to undo the damage."

Hailey had shivered. "It's a wonder he's turned out so special this far." Staring out the window of Mary Jo's apartment, she had focused on the spot where her car should have been—but wasn't.

Her cousin laid a loving hand on her shoulder. "Sammy's okay because you've spent your entire life running interference. You made sure he had lots of love and confidence. Friends and interests."

"I hated leaving him."

"You won't be apart for long. Look, if I had the cash on hand, I swear it'd be yours. Buck says he's about to score big. Maybe I could convince him to…"

Hailey stiffened. "I won't take his money."

Mary Jo stepped away, dropping her hand to her side. "Then this is all you've got. One night can save your entire future."

Unfortunately, Mary Jo had been right. Hailey had no choice. Two days ago, she'd made the final break from her manipulative aunt, taking the last of her life's savings—the fifteen hundred Grace had yet to steal from their joint account—and headed toward a new life. A day later, she'd been carjacked. Gun-wielding teenagers stole her car, her cash, her costumes and worst of all, her precarious sense of safety, leaving her with nothing but the clothes she'd worn and the fifty dollars she'd tucked in her bra. For emergencies.

She couldn't even laugh at the irony.

In those horrifying seconds, her lifelong dream of independence and normality for herself and her brother abruptly ended. Or, at least, hit an abyss even the bus from *Speed* couldn't jump. She'd walked away with her life, but what kind of life would that be?

If she didn't earn at least five hundred dollars by Monday, she'd lose the four thousand she'd deposited a month before as a down payment on her studio. Her career as a dance therapist would go bankrupt before she printed her first business card.

Most importantly, she would have no way of supporting her brother once he left their aunt's house. He'd given her less than a month to get on her feet before he swore he'd run away from Gracie to join her. Sixteen and sensitive, Sammy wasn't the type of kid who'd thrive on the streets. He was an academic whiz kid who needed to worry about school and his future—not about their next meal.

That was Hailey's job. Always had been.

Now, Hailey needed help and Mary Jo offered in the only way she knew. Having run away from Grace herself at eighteen, Mary Jo knew despair firsthand. She'd survived by taking any job she could. When stripping rescued Mary Jo from homelessness, Hailey pushed her preconceived notions aside.

Women in desperate situations did desperate things—just as Hailey would to save her future.

Though separated from Hailey for the past decade, Mary Jo picked Hailey up off her doorstep, offered her a private stripping job and gave her a place to live while she left town with Buck. She'd even negotiated a higher price than usual because they'd tailored the act to the customer's specifications. She may not have had a dollar to her name, but Mary Jo had a big heart.

And a big price. Charging five hundred dollars for each job, plus fifty extra to travel outside Tampa, Mary Jo should have had a stash of savings surpassing the dance contest winnings Aunt Gracie swindled from Hailey. After meeting her boyfriend Buck, however, Hailey suspected Mary Jo's earnings probably paid for more than just his imitation suede jacket and pungent musk cologne.

She also knew he wouldn't put up with Hailey as a third roommate much longer.

Even if she had to prance around in her panties, Hailey wouldn't end up like Mary Jo in one respect—dependent on a man to make her feel important. She'd learned the futility of that from Paul. She'd been so young when they met. Barely sixteen. He'd become her dance partner, her confidant, her protection from Aunt Gracie's constant criticism.

On her eighteenth birthday, he'd become her lover. He showered her with intimate attention, filling her with a sense of power that, with her past, acted almost like a drug. She'd never been with anyone but him and he used her inexperience to keep her under his control. More subtle in his domination than Gracie, Paul managed to direct nearly every aspect of her life without her really taking notice.

Until he left. He abandoned her just months before the most important competition of her career—one whose payout would have financed the education she so desperately wanted to complete.

Since then, every decision she'd made, from finding another partner and finishing college, to leaving Miami and leasing the studio in Tampa, was a bold step toward sweet freedom for her and Sammy.

And sometimes, to find the honeyed center, you have to chew through the bitter edges.

"Two minutes are up, lady," the cabdriver announced. "I gotta get goin'."

Hailey tossed the fifty-dollar bill into the front seat

and closed her coat tighter. "So do I. God help me, but so do I."

When the cab's taillights faded, the early fall of evening cloaked Hailey as she slipped through the unlocked gate and down the palm-lined drive. Mary Jo's customer asked that her arrival be a surprise, not for the groom, oddly enough, but for the owner of the house who reportedly didn't know this gathering was a bachelor party.

Hailey's hopes brightened. Maybe she'd get thrown out before she took off her overcoat. She could demand full payment for her trouble and escape with her self-respect and costume fully intact.

Yet when she crossed in front of the living room picture window, her optimism deflated. Four men in their early thirties congregated around a large screen television, tossing catcalls at a porno film like prison inmates on conjugal visiting day.

Five hundred dollars, she reminded herself. *Without the cash, you're either on the street or slinking back to Aunt Gracie with your tail between your legs. And what about Sammy? He's a lost lamb in a wolf's den without you.*

She raised her hand to the doorbell, but held back when she heard a male voice echo from the side of the house. Deep-throated and controlled, the sound piqued her curiosity.

"I apologize, Mr. Phipps. You were saying?"

Stepping quietly across the portico, she peeked through the branches of a tall rhododendron, spying movement near a set of French doors. High-voltage brass lamps bathed the marble deck in bright light, casting the man, whose voice she'd heard, in shadow. When he stepped out of the glare, her breath caught, not because he might see her, but because he was the most gorgeous—and the most intense-looking—man she'd ever encountered.

Dressed in khaki pants and a golf shirt, he jammed one hand into his pocket. The other clutched the portable phone so tightly, she thought he might crack the casing. His light-brown hair, cropped short and wavy, curved around a face singularly attractive despite his deep-set scowl.

This was a man to be reckoned with, a man of great power. Whoever had wrenched an apology from him just a moment ago must be very, very important.

Hailey'd never really known any men of consequence, but she'd seen them. On television. In the business section of the *Miami Herald*. Featured on the covers of *Money* or *Forbes*. Of course, none had been as devastatingly handsome.

His eyes, dark and intense, reflected utter exasperation. His nose, slanted to bring attention to full grimacing lips, flared at the nostrils, reminding her of a lion disturbed from his nap. His evening was obviously going as swimmingly as hers.

Yet he still managed to look like a god.

And not a minor deity like Theseus or Adonis. An Olympian. A son of Zeus himself.

Hailey shook herself, noting this was the worst possible time for her to find herself in the throes of lust. Lust led to men and men led to trouble. Paul had been a prime example.

This man, however, lacked Paul's spurious sparkle and spit-shine. When he stalked silently from one end of the deck to the other, she warmed at the raw earthiness beneath the casual clothes. Holding his anger in check obviously took every ounce of his concentration, but the strain only enhanced his allure. He looked neither kind nor caring nor loving.

Still, her mouth watered.

He took a step toward the railing. She flattened herself against the outer wall.

"Mr. Phipps, I am not having a 'wild party.'"

Not yet, you're not. Hailey stepped back, finally realizing she couldn't go through with her plan. Alternatives flew through her brain like an Irishman's footwork in a fast-paced jig. Maybe she could work something out with the studio's landlord. After all, she'd already given the man four thousand in cash. She'd get a job—doing anything but stripping—until she could afford the rent. The studio had lots of windows. She could do without air-conditioning for a while. Lettuce was cheap. She'd live on salads—kick that junk-food habit she'd been trying to break. That ought to save a few bucks. In a short time, she'd arrange for patients and start her career.

Then there was Sammy. Hailey drew her thumbnail into her mouth and bit down hard. She couldn't leave him with Grace any longer than she'd planned, but she also couldn't bring him to Tampa until her cash flow improved. Sammy thrived at school with his techno-nerd friends and science courses.

Science course. Hailey remembered Mr. Finch, Sammy's favorite teacher, who'd shown such compassion when she'd gone to the high school to discuss leaving Sammy behind. Knowing Grace's crazy priorities for her niece and nephew, Mr. Finch volunteered to take Sammy in if things with Grace got too crazy. At the time, Hailey had been too proud to accept. The separation was supposed to be temporary and only one month remained until Sammy finished eleventh grade.

Yet things had definitely changed. Finch's sincere offer probably still stood. She'd call him tonight—as soon as she got out of this mess without ruining her or Mary Jo's reputation.

She'd simply ring the doorbell, tell them "Moana," Mary Jo's stage persona, had to go out of town due to an emergency and couldn't perform.

Why was she there? Moana took her commitments seriously, she'd explain. Moana just wanted to make sure they knew she canceled and *couldn't* find a replacement.

Why didn't she just phone? Lost the number.

Yeah, that'll do it.

Then she'd ask them to call her a cab. Nix that. No cash. She'd walk. She'd run. She'd get the hell out of here pronto.

Apollo on the porch would never even know she'd been there.

"Riordan, are you listening?"

On the terrace, Grant Riordan tucked the portable phone under his chin and peered through the French doors. His brother, Gus, and best friend, Mac, sat on the couch inside, glued to a video of the 1983 Superbowl that lit up the large screen. On the floor in front of the TV, Steve, Mike and Tom let out a whoop and a few catcalls.

Must have been a good play.

"Riordan?"

"I apologize, Mr. Phipps. You were saying?"

Reluctantly, he moved from the doors toward the white iron railing. How much trouble could his friends cause in ten unsupervised minutes?

The Chairman of the Board's gruff rasp jerked Grant's focus back to the phone. "Mrs. Langley across the street from you called, during my dinner, and said that an inordinate number of cars are parked in your driveway. She suspects a wild party, just the kind of ripe fodder that woman lines her newspaper column with. Would you care to explain?"

Langley. The battle-ax probably had her binoculars trained on him right now. Grant faced her house across the street and waved.

"Mr. Phipps, I am not having a 'wild party.'"

He considered objecting to Mrs. Langley's nosiness, but held his tongue. The gossip columnist for the *Citrus Hill Weekly* would just claim her First Amendment rights—with a sly wink and a Mae West pat to her silvery hair. The woman thrived on threatening Howell Phipps with another column at his company's expense. Grant suspected Phipps had bought the corporate mansion directly across the street from his nemesis solely for the purpose of baiting her.

Reluctantly, Grant had agreed to the Board of Directors' insistence that he live in the corporate mansion for the first year of his tenure—under the watchful eyes of Wilhelmina Langley and her poison word processor. Since he never did anything scandalous anyway, he hadn't complained. However, he made a mental note to leave his front floodlights on all night. It drove Langley bonkers.

The delightfully juvenile plan vanished when Howell Phipps's bark increased in volume. "Then how would you characterize this 'get-together,' Riordan?"

Grant heard the doorbell and stepped back toward the French doors. Hadn't everyone already arrived? He hadn't seen headlights in the driveway. Maybe the chime he'd heard was a TV commercial.

"Mr. Phipps, you know Steve Ellis, our junior broker who is getting married this weekend?"

"Of course. My wife and I are attending the ceremony."

Oh, great.

"As best man, I've invited the groomsmen over to discuss last-minute preparations."

The silence on the other end of the phone intensified as the music from the house grew louder.

George Thorogood's "Bad To The Bone."

Grant backed from the door. "Mr. Phipps?"

"Good God, Riordan, you're not hosting a bachelor party?"

"Of course not," Grant insisted, annoyed. Didn't the man know that Grant Riordan *never* had fun? Wasn't that why Phipps hired him—along with his money-making expertise?

A bachelor party? He hadn't even gone to his own eight years ago. Camille had dragged him out of town at the last minute to avoid his own prewedding celebration. Even after his divorce, he'd avoided such parties. They reminded him too much of what his life lacked.

"A bachelor party is not my style, Mr. Phipps."

Phipps coughed uncomfortably. "Well, we at First Investment can't be too careful. Your predecessor…"

Grant held the receiver away from his ear. He didn't need to listen, again, as Phipps outlined the sins of CEOs past. The Chairman had already engraved the sordid history into Grant's memory. The most recent Chief Executive Officer had paid off a local madam with investors' funds. The one before him was caught on security videotape having sex with his secretary. In the boardroom. On the table. At lunchtime. Both stories broke in Wilhelmina Langley's weekly column.

Phipps wrapped up his lecture just as Grant spied movement inside the house. Suspicious movement.

"Mr. Phipps, it's eight-thirty on a Thursday night. I'm serving Cabernet Sauvignon, 1986, and the caviar canapés my housekeeper is famous for. My brother brought a tape of his favorite football game in an attempt to liven things up."

"Then you won't object to my stopping by in an hour or so to drop off the papers you'll need for the Board meeting tomorrow?"

Grant's stomach churned. For the umpteenth time, he reminded himself that he needed this job. His income paid for the contractors refurbishing his grandmother's home—a sprawling Victorian he'd grown to love as much as the eighty-two-year-old, newly wheelchair-bound woman who still lived there. Only he and a hefty salary, as well as his weekly visits, guaranteed she'd spend her final days in the only home she'd ever known. Two years ago, he could have financed a complete restoration without feeling the slightest pinch.

Then came Camille and her high-powered divorce attorney.

Just six more months—a year, tops.

Grant's plan was foolproof. His ample paychecks paid the contractors. The location allowed him to visit Nanna Lil regularly. His stock options, coupled with his own undeniable talent for making money, would soon reduce his Camille-induced poverty to nothing but a bitter memory.

He need only stay employed.

"You're more than welcome to stop by, Mr. Phipps. I'll see you in an hour."

"What could possibly go wrong?" Grant muttered once he'd broken the connection.

Opening the doors, Grant choked on his words.

He didn't follow the game, but Grant knew the contact sport on the screen wasn't football. That type of huddle didn't happen in the NFL—at least, not on the field. The term "redskins" took on a whole new meaning.

The porno tape was the least of his worries. No longer interested in the video, his buddies congregated near the CD player. Raucous guitar licks and pounding bass from the surround-sound speakers rattled the crystal chandelier. Rowdy whoops from his cohorts added to the clamor. Grant slammed the door behind him, crossed the threshold into the living room, and dropped the phone. Then his jaw.

His friends weren't whooping at the CD player, but at a petite brunette, dressed in a trench coat, who looked like a deer caught in a hunter's headlights.

Grant's mouth lost all moisture. Her wide eyes, the shade of sparkling blue topaz, sought his with an unspoken plea for help. Only the fact that he'd never seen her before, and he knew his friends to be harmless, kept him from immediately rushing to her aid.

"Moana couldn't work tonight. She sent me to tell you." She spoke the words directly to him, as if she hoped he'd react since the others preferred ogling to listening.

"Aw, come on, honey." Steve slurred, a half-empty beer in one hand, his other pawing at her belt. She stepped back and clutched her coat by the lapels, but not before he managed to slip the canvas tie from its loops. "We gotta have some entertainment."

Entertainment? Suddenly, the trench coat made sense. A sickening sensation coiled in his stomach. The gorgeous female fantasy on the other side of his living room was a stripper. And a terrified one at that.

When Steve latched on to the hem of her coat and began reeling her forward, Grant bolted across the room. If Langley caught wind of this, or worse, if Phipps showed up early...*if Steve touched her again*...he pushed the thought away and jumped over Mac, aiming for her discarded belt. Gus grabbed Grant's ankle, knocking him off balance. As he stumbled, he avoided an open cooler of beer partially shoved under his Queen Anne coffee table.

The fall sent him rolling toward the stripper, who jerked from his path. Her shoulders crashed into the CD player, teetering the tall, glass bookshelf.

Men shouted. The woman screamed. Knickknacks tumbled down like porcelain rain. In a clumsy attempt to help Grant up, Mac fell on top of him. Steve and Tom erupted in laughter. Gus belched.

Amid the chaos, a polyurethane-sealed book hidden on the top shelf pummeled down. Right on the stripper's head.

And knocked her out cold.

2

"OH, GREAT," GUS lamented. "She hadn't even taken off her coat."

Grant squirmed from under Mac and crawled to the stripper. She was definitely unconscious, and despite the snug leather pants and jacket peeking through her coat, bold makeup and blue-black hair, she looked peaceful. Innocent.

Carefully, Grant touched the back of her head and felt a lump. *Damn.* "She's hurt. Help me get her to the couch."

"I'll call 9-1-1," Mac said, suddenly serious and sober.

"Now you decide to act like a cop?" Grant snapped. "Where was your blue sense when you let this woman in?" *Lord, he could just imagine Langley's take on police cars and paramedics.*

"Just hold on. Don't move her till I look at her. Get my bag, Tom," Gus ordered, suddenly authoritative as his Hippocratic oath overpowered his hormones. "In the front seat of my car."

"No," Grant amended, shifting so his thighs cushioned the stripper's head. "Mac, you get the bag. Tom, you and Mike get Steve out of here."

His inebriated friend, although deserving of a little fun on the eve of his wedding, suddenly angered Grant just by being there. He didn't want the junior broker in his living room when Phipps arrived. Drunk and obnoxious, Steve could ruin his own career—and Grant's.

The boiling he felt in his blood undoubtedly stemmed from that possibility. His anger had nothing to do with the way Steve had pawed the stripper. Nothing at all.

Mac led the others out while Gus checked the stripper's bump and then her pulse. Her raven hair, cut in a stylish shag, brushed Grant's hand with a lacy texture. He untangled an errant strand from her long eyelashes.

"She's all twisted in this coat and jacket. She's probably burning up," Gus said. "I'll lean her forward. Slip her arms out."

"I don't think that's necessary." After the glimpse Grant had of the clothing she wore beneath her modest London Fog knock-off, he knew his libido couldn't endure a fuller view.

Gus unfastened her buttons and unzipped the jacket underneath. "Who's the doctor here, you or me?"

"At this point, it's debatable." Reluctantly, Grant did as Gus asked. Try as he did not to look when his brother removed her coat and jacket, his gaze traveled over her leather-encased body with aching slowness. She was small, no more than five foot four, but feminine curves and softly toned muscles filled all the right places in all the right ways. Her low-cut bustier and spray-painted pants revealed more about this woman than a stranger had a right to see.

Taking the coat off was bad enough. Taking the jacket off was a big mistake. Oh, yeah. A whopper.

Mac returned with the bag, stumbling when he caught sight of the increasingly undressed stripper. "Hot damn."

Grant shoved him away. "You're married, remember?"

Mac jammed his hands deep into his pockets. "Marriage doesn't kill every man's lust."

"Camille didn't kill my lust. It died from neglect," Grant answered.

"Okay, boys, step aside." Gus rolled up his sleeves. "Give the doctor room."

"Some doctor. You're a podiatrist," Grant said.

"Med school is med school," Gus asserted. "Grab a pillow from the couch."

Grant followed Gus's instructions as he examined the beautiful young scandal crumpled on the living room floor. Grant mentally kicked himself, glancing furtively out of the front window and checking his watch. What could possibly go wrong? *Sure, Mr. Phipps, come on over. Join the party.* The overzealous moans from the videotape nearly drove him mad. He found the remote amid a stack of dog-eared, contraband *Hustler* magazines and switched the television off.

"Grant, I need an ice pack. She's coming around."

He returned just in time to see her sit up and grab the back of her head in pain.

"Ow," she groaned.

Gus took the pack from Grant and pressed the cold blue gel against the swelling bump.

"Hold this," Gus said. "I need to check your pupils."

When the ice pack slipped out of her shaking hand, Grant slid behind her and held it himself. The warm scent of mulled spice nearly sent him reeling.

Her eyes glazed with fear. "Who are you? What happened?"

"You might have a slight concussion," Gus informed her.

She blinked away from his penlight. "Concussion? From what? Where am I?" Jerking from Gus's touch, she slammed into Grant's chest, which sent her scrambling in the other direction. Terror marred her lovely face, glossing her blue eyes with tell-tale moisture. "Who are you people?"

She tried to stand, but her knees wobbled and she fell into Grant's arms. He braced her against his chest, caught another whiff of her rich cinnamon perfume, and nearly lost his balance.

"Let go of me." She pushed weakly against his chest, until her protests were quickly spent. "My head."

"Bring her to the couch," Gus instructed.

Stepping over the litter of leather and beer cans, Grant led her to the couch farthest from the drapeless picture window. He tried not to inhale the scent wafting from her skin, tried not to feast on the generous swell of her breasts pressed against tight black leather.

He couldn't help himself.

Gus gathered his bag and spoke calmly to his patient. "Miss, can you tell me your name?"

She answered him with a blank stare. Shock, mingled with near-panic, defied her makeup and turned her skin an ashy white.

Gus slipped his penlight back into his bag. "Oh, boy."

Grant's ulcer burned. He'd thought the ailment had disappeared forever the day he'd left Wall Street. And Camille. But no. He had a captivating stripper on his couch who couldn't remember her name, a semidrunk podiatrist treating her head injury, and a nosy pseudojournalist across the street who could destroy his career with one phone call. Stomach acid churned like an active volcano.

"'Oh, boy?' What does that mean, Gus?" Grant's voice deepened as he lost hold of his calm. He gulped in air to steady his increasing rage.

Gus shot his brother a frustrated "not now" look and returned to his interrogation. "Do you know where you are?"

Anxiety shone in her eyes until they gleamed like faceted sapphires. She glanced about furtively, as if not wanting them to see how thirstily she drank in the details of her surroundings. She studied her palms as she spoke. "I'm here, with you. Do *you* know where *we* are?"

"We're at my brother's house," Gus answered calmly. "Do you know *why* we're here?"

The woman sat up, looked at her clothing, then again at the overturned furnishings, the cooler of beer, her discarded coat.

"Looks like a party. Was I invited?"

"No," Grant snapped.

Gus socked him on the arm like when they were kids.

"Yes," Gus corrected. "You were the entertainment."

She stared blankly at him again. "And I do…"

Waiting for them to fill in the blanks, she looked expectantly at all three of them. Mac turned away, probably wondering how he'd explain his involvement with a stripper to his lieutenant. Gus ran his meaty hands through his prematurely thinning hair. Grant folded his arms over his chest and scrutinized her. She truly had no idea what she did for a living.

Oh, Lord.

"You're a stripper," he provided matter-of-factly.

Her eyebrows shot up beneath her bangs. "That explains the draft."

Mac handed her jacket to Grant, who draped the thin leather across her shoulders. She pulled the sleeves quickly out of his hands, then yanked the ice pack away.

"Would someone please tell me why I can't remember anything?"

"You were bumped on the head." Gus leaned around her to check the swelling. "The concussion isn't too serious, but you seem to have amnesia. It's probably temporary. Can you recall your name yet?"

"Who hired me?"

"I did," Gus admitted.

"Then why don't you tell me my name and we can quit the twenty questions?"

Grant fought the impulse to smile. Even at her most vulnerable, this woman proved tough. Not like the women he'd been attracted to before—no siree. There'd be no inane small talk or veiled innuendoes with this woman. Once she regained her strength, she'd probably tell him to shove his warped country-club morality and high-society values where the sun didn't shine.

Straightening from his crouched position beside the couch, Gus dug his hands into his pockets. "I can't tell you your name. That's not how amnesia works."

"There are rules?" she asked.

Gus glanced up evasively, then away from Grant's scowl. "It's better if you remember naturally. Besides," he admitted sheepishly, "I don't know who you are."

"What?"

The woman and Grant stared at each other, amazed as their question rang out in unison.

"What do you mean you don't know who she is? Gus, you hired her," Grant pointed out.

"No, I hired someone else."

"Who?"

This time, the stripper beat him to the question.

Grant watched as, with effort, his brother forced his brain to work through a beer-enhanced haze. "Um…Moana, yeah, Moana was the name she danced under."

The woman's eyebrows creased together. "Moana? Moana." She blew out a frustrated breath. "I don't recognize the name." Grabbing her cheeks with quivering hands, she shook her head, wincing. "I don't recognize anything."

Mac stepped forward, knelt on one knee and patted her arm. "Just stay calm, okay? We're going to help you."

The woman didn't seem to hear Mac's assurance. Grant's heart lurched, the sensation quickly followed by a sickening wave of foreboding. He couldn't allow himself to imagine the confusion swimming in her mind, to feel the loss so evident in her eyes. He couldn't let himself be a sucker for a pretty face in a desperate situation. That's what irresponsible, impulsive men with a "knight in shining armor" complex did. Not Grant Riordan, Mr. Responsible Extraordinaire.

He turned his attention to Gus. "Where did you meet Moana? If we can find her…"

"I've known Moana off and on for years. Last time I saw her she worked at the Cat House in Orlando, I think. Or was it Pretty Maids in Tampa, or Deceptions down on the strip?"

Grant threw up his hands and retreated, busying himself with searching for undamaged figurines on the plush carpet while trying to ignore his brother as he recited the names of numerous strip clubs, none of which seemed familiar to the woman on the couch. Gus frequented so many clubs, the chances of him remembering exactly where he'd seen Moana last were as slim as Grant keeping his job past midnight.

"Do you still have her number?" Grant asked, frustrated by their slow progress as much as by his inability to stop staring at the stripper's seductive blue eyes or trembling bottom lip.

Shaking his head, Gus answered, "Maybe at the office. I confirmed with Moana a week ago, and then she called me day before yesterday to jack up her price."

The stripper turned away, obviously trying to hide the glisten of moisture in her eyes. Unfortunately, Grant hadn't missed a single sparkle. He couldn't believe she hadn't succumbed to tears yet—either out of the desperation of her situation or to gain the upper hand.

Not that she needed tears for that. This little incident had "lawsuit" written all over it in bold, red letters. First Investment would have its next sex scandal—and Grant faced financial ruin.

But instead of crying or threatening legal action, she took a deep, steadying breath, braced herself on the couch and stood. "Where's the little stripper's room? Maybe a splash of water will clear my head."

Mac led her toward the hallway, pointing out the door beneath the staircase.

Grant gazed at her, speechless—as much from her outward calm as from the sensual way her hips swayed when she walked. After she disappeared, he grabbed Gus by the shirt.

"Now what are you going to do, Mr. 'Med-School-is-Med-School?' Phipps'll be here any minute."

Gus pulled back, nearly tripping over the coffee table.

"Hey, back off, brother. You want to knock out my memory too?"

Grant didn't stop. "What memory? How could you possibly forget where you knew this Moana person from? If we knew where she came from, we could take little Lady Lawsuit there and drop her off before she sues me."

"She didn't say anything about a lawsuit," Gus reassured him.

"Not yet, she hasn't."

Mac patted Grant on the shoulder. "It was an accident, Grant. You even had the police here to witness the sordid event. She won't file criminal charges."

Grant's cynicism didn't falter. "She could still file a civil suit."

"She'd have to know her name to do that," Gus added.

"Of course, maybe she's faking the amnesia," Mac wondered aloud. He paced once across the living room. "This could be a setup to extort money from Grant."

"Extortion?" Grant, surprised he hadn't considered that scenario himself, clenched Gus's shirt tighter. The stripper didn't *seem* that cruel or conniving. Then again, neither had Camille until they divorced. "Extortion."

Gus pulled his shirt from Grant's clutch. "Get real, Mac. Haven't you ever heard about not taking your job home with you? And you," Gus addressed his brother, "you've been watching too many reruns of *Murder, She Wrote*. I don't think she's faking."

"Is this the professional opinion of a small-town podiatrist?" Grant spat out. "I suppose I can stop worrying now."

"We can still have her checked out at the hospital." Mac snatched the cordless phone from the floor and twirled it by its antenna.

"No, that's too public." Grant knew he was blowing this whole situation out of proportion, but he needed a solution. Fast. He was too close to ending his financial problems and starting fresh to have a farcical twist of fate ruin his carefully laid plans. Besides, having her in such close proximity awakened needs he'd worked a long time to suppress.

"Take her home with you, Gus."

"Excuse me?"

"You're the doctor," Grant reasoned. "You can help her recover."

Gus threw himself on the couch and popped open another beer. "Yeah, yeah, I can see it now." He raised the pitch of his voice to mimic a carefree lilt, "Lisa, honey, I'd like you to meet…well, I don't know who she is, but she's a stripper and she's staying with us for a few days. Why us? Well, you see, I've been frequenting the strip clubs, even though you told me you'd rip my throat out if I did it again, and she—"

"Enough." Grant fell onto the cushions beside his brother and fought the temptation to join him in a brew. He needed a clear head. "Lisa will leave you in a heartbeat if she finds out."

He looked up at Mac.

"Don't even think about it, guys. Even if I had the space in my loft apartment, I don't think Jenna would understand. What about a hotel?"

Grant shook his head. "Where? The Fairway Inn is the only decent place in town and Wilhelmina Langley has a direct line to their front desk. And I doubt if our guest would agree to a room in Tampa or Orlando."

She'd be stupid to agree. In the few short minutes he'd known her, he recognized that this woman was anything but dumb. By taking her to a hotel, especially one in another city, he could wash his hands of her and the whole situation—claim never to have seen her before.

To someone else, the plan might have been perfect. But Grant Riordan practically had "responsibility" tattooed on his forehead.

The facts lay like a diving red arrow on a profits graph. Mac and Gus couldn't help. Grant had nowhere to keep the mystery woman except with him. At least, until she recovered her memory.

"Oh!" The distinctly feminine moan beckoned the three men to the kitchen like an alarm.

They stopped dead in the doorway. Bent at the waist as she explored the contents of the refrigerator, the stripper offered a tantalizing view of her leather-clad backside. Grant felt a stirring in his groin. A man in his position couldn't possibly be attracted to her, could he?

Sure, he could. His American red blood ran as hot as any other man's—maybe hotter since he'd kept his needs bottled up since his disastrous divorce. Hell, he'd kept his needs imprisoned since he'd headed down the aisle. Maybe before. And now, practically gift-wrapped in black leather and needing his help, his perfect fantasy lover stood in his kitchen, eyeing his near-empty refrigerator as if it were a smorgasbord.

Before he delved further into the details of his fantasy, he strode forward and pulled her away from the door. Only then did he notice how she clutched the back of her head.

"Aren't you cold, staring into the refrigerator?"

Startled by his presence, she crossed her arms defiantly, her wrists cradling the lower swell of her breasts.

"My head hurts. I thought a little food would help and I didn't want to interrupt you."

He released her, struck once again by her transparent honesty. If this woman was orchestrating a scam, he was a twenty-year veteran of the Hell's Angels.

"I should have offered. Let me fix you something."

Her smile lit her eyes like bursting stars. "I'll take some wine and caviar. You've got quite a selection."

Grant smirked at her disguised gibe, knowing his refrigerator held only a few staples in addition to the "entertaining" food he had purchased for tonight. Yet before he could respond to her sarcasm, Gus escorted her to the kitchen dinette.

"No wine for you, missy. You need rest. Your memory could return at any time. Most amnesia cases from a minor bump to the head are temporary."

"What about the fish eggs?"

Grant huffed quietly, then retrieved the caviar.

"Fish eggs are fine if you're not feeling nauseous," Gus said, "but what if Grant whips them into one of his famous omelets? We'll wash it down with some healthy orange juice."

Now this is a turn of events. First, he's practically forced into playing host to the woman. Now he's her short-order cook? He tried to be annoyed, but the feeling wouldn't take root—until he glanced at his watch. Phipps would arrive in less than thirty minutes.

"Would you like bacon with that?" he asked.

"No pork flesh, thank you." She kicked her high-heeled, calf-hugging, lace-up boots onto the chair across from her.

As Gus politely asked her questions, none of which she could answer, Grant banged around the kitchen in search of pots and pans. She couldn't remember how she arrived. A cab? A friend? The buses didn't run in Grant's neighborhood after six o'clock. Mac listened from the doorway until his beeper went off and he retreated to the other room to call his precinct.

Grant cracked eggs into a metal bowl. "So, what should we call you, since you can't remember your name?"

When she didn't answer, he glanced over his shoulder.

She stared at her open palms. When she looked up at him, her azure eyes gleamed with disappointment. "You think I'm lying, don't you?"

He'd met many a conniving woman in his life, one in particular that he'd married, but the hurt in this woman's voice was genuine. He immediately wished he'd softened his accusatory tone. "You've fallen into a pretty great setup."

"Yeah, right. Before I got here, I knew I'd get hit on the head by a..." Her voice trailed off. "What, or who—" she glanced dubiously at Grant "—hit me anyway?"

Just as she asked the question, Mac entered the kitchen with the offending sealed book in hand and a Cheshire-cat grin on his face. "You were assaulted by the illustrated *Kama Sutra*. An *unopened* copy."

Grant dashed for the book, tearing the thick tome out of Mac's hands before he and Gus completely lost themselves to snickers. The stripper didn't say a word.

"A parting gift from Camille," he explained loudly as he marched back into the living room and replaced the book on the top shelf. When he returned, he took relish in beating the eggs to a golden froth. "She always had a sick sense of humor."

"No, she didn't." Gus swigged from the beer he still held. "If she did, I would have liked her. She was just trying to psych you out."

"Who's Camille?" The stripper sipped her juice, but eyed Gus's beer longingly.

"His ex," Gus answered. "She left for Europe two

years ago, and since then, the colonies have been a happier place.''

The room grew quiet until Mac blurted out, "Harley.''

"What?'' Grant asked. The stripper stared at her glass as if she hadn't heard.

"Yeah, that's it!'' Gus agreed, elated. He stood and raised his hand to Mac in a high-five, sitting abashedly when his friend failed to join in.

Grant and the woman stared at each other, both missing the significance.

"Mac, what are you talking about?'' Grant asked.

"I didn't remember till now, but when she first came in, she said her name was Harley. It just popped back into my head because of my phone call. One of my informants has a tip on a carjacking motorcycle gang I've been trailing. I'm meeting him in an hour.''

The men looked at her expectantly, but she shrugged her shoulders. "I suppose that could be my name. 'Harley.' Sounds strippy enough. Hey, did I have any identification? A purse or a wallet?''

Mac retrieved her coat from the living room. "Nothing in here.''

She stood and checked her costume for pockets while Grant kept his attention on the sizzling omelet. He succeeded for about thirty seconds. He couldn't resist watching Harley frisk herself. She patted her breasts and hips in quick motions—exactly the opposite of how he'd proceed if he were conducting her full body search. He'd move slowly, careful to investigate every curve, curious to discover the origin of each and every swell.

When she lifted her foot onto her chair to explore the insides of her zipped boot, she paused, as if she'd spied him watching in her peripheral vision. A faint pink blush bloomed above her breasts.

Grant snapped his attention back to the pan just as the eggs turned a golden brown, a shade darker than he preferred. So the omelet would be a little overdone. It was her own damn fault.

Harley sat and blew out a pent-up breath. "Nothing."

Mac glanced at his watch. "When I get back to the precinct, I'll check the computer's missing persons network and take a look at Vice priors for anyone named Harley or using it as an alias."

"Can that be done quietly?" Grant slid the cooked omelet onto a plate.

"No one has to know," Mac reassured. "The file is updated regularly. Someone's bound to report her missing."

"Oh, wait." Harley jumped from her seat with her juice. She dumped the orange liquid into the sink and extended the glass to Mac. "Can't you take my fingerprints from this glass? I think I saw it on TV once."

"Another *Murder, She Wrote* fan," Gus quipped. "Don't you people know anything about viewer demographics?"

Setting the plate at Harley's empty place, Grant felt a jabbing pang of guilt. Her pride was unmistakable. If this were a scam, would she have been so eager to provide something as surefire as fingerprints?

Mac placed the glass in a plastic bag he pulled from the pantry. "I have a friend in the lab. I'll see what I can do. In the meantime," he addressed Grant, "call the local cab company and see if anyone drove out here tonight. If she came from Tampa or Orlando, tracking her point of origin could be tough. Both cities have over a dozen cab companies. I'll call you at the office tomorrow."

"No." Grant needed to keep any mention of Harley out of the office. "Leave a message on my home machine."

After seeing Mac out and reinforcing the importance of total confidentiality, Grant returned to the kitchen to find Gus and Harley sharing the omelet. Laughing quietly with his brother, she didn't look the least bit like a stripper. Sure, her clothes were provocative and she wore her makeup in daring streaks, but the lack of guile in her blue eyes and the sweetness of her smile seemed too natural and unsophisticated for a woman in her profession.

Then again, what did he know about strippers? He hadn't been in a strip club since college, and since he'd usually gone with his younger brother, he'd never allowed himself to enjoy the experience. He was the older brother. The responsible one. The boring one.

Or did he mean "bored"?

"You staying the night, Gus?" Grant asked, only half hopeful his brother would accept. "I have guest rooms in this house I haven't even seen yet."

Gus pushed away from the table. "Thanks, bro, but my night isn't over yet. I'm going to stop by the office and look around for that number. You, my dear," he addressed Harley in a surprisingly fatherly tone, "need rest. Except for a nasty bump and your amnesia, you don't have any serious symptoms. You'll probably remember everything by morning."

His smile was reassuring. Grant prayed his brother was right.

"Thanks, Doc," Harley said. "I'm sorry I've caused so much trouble."

Gus shook her proffered hand. "No trouble."

Grant coughed.

"Okay, maybe a little trouble. But this is the most fun I've had in months. Just the look on Grant's face…"

A glance at Grant's unamused expression stopped Gus's explanation dead cold.

"Call me if your headache gets worse," he instructed, and then to Grant said, "Keep an eye on her. If she becomes dizzy or her pupils dilate, call 9-1-1 or take her to the emergency room."

Grant nodded, then escorted Gus to the front door.

"You okay to drive?" Grant asked once they reached the foyer.

Gus patted his pants until he found his keys. "Actually, I've never felt more sober."

"Having your brother on the verge of killing you can do that to a man," Grant quipped.

Gus slapped him on the shoulder. "Come on, Grant. You have a beautiful young babe staying with you tonight. A great scenario in my book."

Grant preferred not to consider that "scenario," though he did wonder how she'd look first thing in the morning, with the makeup scrubbed off and her hair in dreamy disarray. He shoved his hands into his pockets and cleared his throat. "I'll expect a phone call as soon as possible."

"Sure thing, bro." Gus shuffled over to a desk in the foyer and pulled out a slip of stationery, scribbled, then folded the note as he spoke. "Wake her up once or twice tonight."

Grant raised his eyebrows. Several delightful ways of waking a beautiful woman like Harley flashed in his mind. One corner of his mouth tilted to a grin.

Gus slapped his hand over his heart. "Excuse me, but did my celibate brother just entertain a sexual thought?"

Grant stuffed his hands deeper into his pockets and frowned. "I did not. And I'm not celibate. I just…"

"Yeah, yeah, must have been gas. It's okay for her to sleep, but wake her up a couple of times and ask if she remembers who and where she is. It's just a precaution. Here's a list of things to do if you have any minor problems."

Grant nodded and stuffed the tightly folded paper into his shirt pocket.

Retrieving his bag, Gus stopped at the threshold. "Don't do anything I wouldn't do."

Grant pushed his brother through the open front door. "Just exactly what does that *not* include?"

Without waiting for an answer, Grant slammed the door and surveyed the damage in the living room. He picked up the remnants of two shattered Lladro porcelains, then quickly shoved the empty beer cans and porno magazines into the garbage, hung Harley's trench coat in the back of the hall closet and returned the throw pillows to their places. On his way back to the kitchen, he glanced out the picture window, turned on the front floodlights and smiled.

Take that, Langley.

Grant checked his watch once more. Luckily for him, Phipps was probably too much of a gentleman to arrive early. He hastened to the kitchen to escort his unexpected houseguest upstairs.

She stood at the sink, washing the omelet pan. She'd discarded the leather jacket and bustier, leaving only the thin-strapped bikini top and tight pants. Steam rose from the faucet. When she turned to retrieve the plate from the table, her skin shimmered with moisture.

He couldn't prevent taking a few steps closer. The circular motions of her soapy hands seemed oddly sensual. When she slipped her fingers inside a wineglass, he cleared his throat.

She glanced over her shoulder.

"So, banker-boy. When do we go to bed?"

3

"PARDON ME?"

Harley regretted her words the minute she witnessed the darkening of his eyes. The rich shade of milk chocolate, his gaze melted down the length of her body. She squirmed and leaned away until her back, bare since she'd discarded her jacket and bustier in the heat of the kitchen, met with the water she'd dripped on the edge of the sink.

Once again, anxiety held her speechless.

When she'd retreated to the bathroom earlier to splash water on her face, she'd succumbed to a similar frenzy of fear. Who was she? Why did she strip for a living? Was she desperate for cash? On drugs? A mother with hungry children to feed? She had no answers, and wouldn't get any as long as terror tangled her brain. So instead, she concentrated on what she did know.

Her host would help her, however reluctantly. Her presence alone was a trump card, one she'd play until she regained her memory. He wouldn't hurt her. Amid his blatant desire, empathy warmed his cocoa-tinted eyes.

"You heard the doc." Regaining her composure, she swallowed deeply and walked toward him. Heat rose from his flushed skin. In response, every bared inch of her crested with an unfamiliar, yet pleasant warmth. She stopped. She didn't know him. Didn't know herself. Yet, she gravitated toward him like a falling satellite. "I need rest. You look like you could use some sleep yourself."

His Adam's apple bobbed above the V-necked collar of his shirt. "What I need, Miss Harley, is to lead you upstairs before my boss arrives to drop off some important paperwork."

Okay, so they told her Harley was her name, but it didn't sound familiar, especially not with a prim-sounding "Miss" attached.

"Look, banker-boy, the name's Harley. Just Harley. At least until I learn otherwise."

"Fine, Just Harley. And since we're on the topic, my name is Grant Riordan, not 'banker-boy.' I'm not even a banker, for Pete's sake."

Nor was he a boy. When he retrieved a dish towel from a drawer and extended it to her, she noticed the thick, curled brown hair dusting his muscular forearms. He wore a slate-blue golf shirt with short sleeves that accentuated his biceps and showed off his tan.

"Grant, huh?" She grabbed the towel by the loose end, careful not to make contact with his skin—fearing the effect would burn her with an electric shock. "Your name even sounds wealthy. You know, as in 'loan.'" She dried her hands and tossed the towel onto the table.

He retrieved the towel and folded it neatly. "You're not the first person to notice, but my name came from a more…historical source." With surprising ease, he took her into his confidence. "My father is an American history professor."

Harley found his admission, accompanied by a sheepish, half-tilted grin, more beguiling than uppity. He gestured to the door, then waited while she picked up the leather jacket and bustier. The tone of his voice had softened, and the harsh lines of tension faded from his face like midmorning fog. At the same time, Harley's taut nerves eased. She hadn't realized how her shoulders and stomach had cramped from anxiety. She felt, if only momentarily, safe from the unknown.

Safe with a perfect stranger.

"Don't tell me." She followed him into the living room. "You were named for the great Union general."

"The one and only. But I'd appreciate your keeping that under wraps." He stopped midway into the room, peered out the picture window, then leaned toward her conspiratorially. "Many of my investors are Southern retirees."

She chuckled again, then watched as her amusement transferred to him, lighting his face with a slight, yet powerful grin. Though she'd known him for less than an hour, she decided this man should laugh more often.

"My lips are sealed." She twisted her fingers over her mouth as if locking her lips with a key.

For the briefest moment, his gaze lingered longingly on her mouth. When she blinked, he'd turned away. If not for the steady ache at the back of her scalp, she would have shaken some sense into herself. Every gesture, every expression, every nuance of this man's body language garnered her undivided attention. With her own mind blank, did she seek to fill the void with knowledge of him?

The possibility made her quiver.

They passed through the living room, prompting her to consider asking him more about the party. Just how wild had the celebration gotten before the Hindu sex guide clunked her on the head? She glanced around. All remnants of the party had vanished. She had awakened fully dressed. Except for the headache and the apprehension she fought with every step, she felt pretty darn good.

But why was she a stripper? Where did she come from? She stopped and took a deep breath. There was no sense in badgering herself. If she could just relax, her brain might kick into gear on its own. Maybe she'd regain her memories by morning, like the doc said.

Grant motioned upstairs, waiting for her to pass before he followed. She grabbed the handrail and climbed carefully. After reaching the midway point, she realized Grant was several steps below her—undoubtedly at eye level with her backside. A volcanic blush spread over her cheeks, neck and chest.

Some stripper she was, she thought.

"What about the doc?" Harley filled the silence with nervous chatter, hoping he wouldn't notice the reddening of her skin. "I don't remember any valiant generals named Gus."

She stopped when he snickered, and her quick backward glance caught a flash of amusement in his eyes. Deep brown eyes. Sexy eyes. Maybe he'd think her flush came from the exertion of climbing the stairs.

"Father chose my name, since I was born first. However, my brother fell victim to Mother's whim."

"'Gus' is a whim?"

"His real name is Gustave. Mother is a professor of European literature."

"Oh," she said knowingly, "and a student of scandal."

"Pardon me?"

She paused and faced him. "You meant Flaubert, right? Gustave Flaubert? Author of *Madame Bovary*, among others?" Words popped into her head as if she read them from an internal page. "The scintillating story of an underappreciated wife who steps into the sordid world of illicit extramarital affairs."

He nodded, obviously as surprised by her knowledge as she.

"Hey, what do you know?" she said proudly, turning to take the last few steps to the top. "I'm an educated stripper."

The minute she finished the rotation, she knew she'd spun too quickly. Bright light shot from inside her eyelids, and her foot missed the next step.

Grant caught her behind the elbows, his hands big and strong and steady. "Whoa. One injury a night is enough, don't you think?"

His tone was neither disapproving nor accusatory, yet Harley felt compelled to apologize. "Sorry. I guess I'm still a little dizzy."

"That's understandable." He steadied her all the way to the second door from the top of the stairs and didn't release her until she eyed his palms cupping her elbows. He coughed uncomfortably.

He opened the door, leaned in and flicked on the light, then backed away to let her enter. When she passed, he looked aside and shoved his hands in his pockets, unwilling or unable to make eye contact. Suddenly chilled, she crossed her arms and rubbed her elbows precisely where his hands had caught her, missing their warmth.

The room was tasteful, although austere in decor. The limited spectrum of creams and taupes decorated the traditional, whitewashed maple furniture—bed, bureau, nightstand, wardrobe, chaise lounge—and met every need except a creative one.

She summoned the most appropriate description she could muster. "It's, um, nice."

He looked around, his interest indicating he hadn't

been in the room before. Or if he had, he hardly remembered. "This guest room hasn't been used since I moved in, but my housekeeper sees that the linens are changed regularly, just in case." He pointed. "The bathroom is through that door. The closet is there."

She held up her jacket and bustier. "These shouldn't take up too much room."

His gaze dropped to the floor, then returned to her face, stabbing her with sharp disapproval. Or was his expression only mirroring his unease? "I'll find you something to sleep in and I'll arrange for more…casual clothes tomorrow. If we have to."

If we have to. She could regain her memory and be out of his world in just a matter of hours. Why did that bother her? Returning to her own life and anyone who might worry about her, miss her, or need her should fill her with elation. In wanting to stay, she was just clinging to the familiar. The *recently* familiar.

Better a devil she knew. A devil who'd taken her in before she'd even asked.

He left momentarily, returning with a clean T-shirt, a new toothbrush, and a warning to stay in her room when his boss dropped by. As he moved to leave, she shifted her weight from right to left, then willed herself to remain still.

"Grant, wait." She clutched the T-shirt to her chest, somewhat disappointed that she smelled only fabric softener in the smooth white cotton. "I want to thank you. You didn't have to take me in like this."

His eyebrow arched skeptically and his smile tilted only one side of his mouth. "I didn't? What would you have done if I'd tried to throw you out?"

An iced shiver snaked across her midsection, despite how his tone told her he would never have stooped so low as to refuse to help someone who'd lost everything to one bump on the head. Honestly, she didn't know what she would have done. She didn't think she was the cry-'til-you-get-your-way type, nor would she threaten a frivolous lawsuit like the one she'd overheard him mention.

"I suppose I would just have had to appeal to your chivalrous side," she decided.

His smile hinted at a wickedness that sent shock waves throughout her body. "What if I didn't have a chivalrous side?"

She moved to toss her jacket on the bed, then, remembering the dish towel, hung it up instead. "You do. So for that, I'm grateful."

He acknowledged her thanks with a stilted nod, the smile wiped from his lips. He had a chivalrous side, but wasn't the least bit comfortable with it. For a few minutes, she mused over why he'd regret being gallant and gentlemanly, then abruptly stopped. She had her own past to worry about. More than likely, she wouldn't know this man beyond tomorrow morning. Something deep in her gut told her that obsessing over Grant Riordan could lead to nothing but trouble.

She took a quick shower then climbed into bed. Though she adjusted the pillows and indulged in several yawns, sleep remained elusive. The room was too big. Too quiet. The bed too cold and empty.

Fighting the dull throb from her injury, she tried to remember something—anything—about who she was. After the exchange on the stairs, she knew she had probably gone to college, yet she remembered nothing about school.

As for her "career," nothing came to mind. Grant and Gus told her she was a stripper, and she'd certainly dressed like one, but the idea seemed ludicrous. She pulled up the comforter and settled in, trying to picture herself prancing around to some seductive instrumental and peeling her clothes off in front of catcalling, salivating men. She didn't believe she could do such a thing—until that picture focused solely on Grant Riordan.

She imagined shedding her leather in front of him alone. The image darkened as if in a room lit only by colored gels, the music slow and sexy. She fantasized about shimmying out of her snug leather jeans, shrugging out of the jacket and bustier, then leaning over to let him untie the bow of her bikini top.

Then she visualized Grant's face. The fantasy ended. His disapproving frown doused her imagination with stinging cold. Even in her dreams, the man needed to lighten up.

She might not remember anything specific about herself, but Harley decided she was a good and decent person, in spite of her profession. He'd be damned lucky to have her.

With a derisive "humph," Harley snuggled into the pillows. Someplace, somewhere, somebody waited for her. Worried about her. Considered themselves lucky and honored to be her friend. She repeated the mantra in her mind a thousand times, but her heart remained unconvinced. Deep down, and with no proof to present to her malfunctioning mind, Harley feared the dawn. What if she woke up with her memory intact, and learned she was alone in the world?

Or worse, what if she woke up still trapped by amnesia?

Harley finally drifted to sleep, thinking of how she had no one to count on, no one to help her but herself...and the gorgeous stranger in the bedroom down the hall.

GRANT SIMPLY HAD to find somewhere else for her to go. He tossed onto his left shoulder, pounded the pillow with a grunt, and tried to think of some secret place he could stash Harley until her memory returned and he sent her on her merry way. That was, after all, the right thing to do. First Investment couldn't withstand another scandal. Not even a hint of one. The Board members and stockholders were good people who'd put their trust in him. Even though he loathed the pressure, he needed his job long enough to fix Nanna's antiquated house and ensure his own future wealth—wealth some conniving woman couldn't win away by court order.

Harley could ruin his plans with one bump and grind.

Just after Phipps left, Mac had called with the news that no one matching Harley's description had been reported missing, nor did he find her in his computer. Gus still couldn't find Moana's number, though he promised to keep looking. The local taxi service hadn't made any drop-offs in his neighborhood and the two largest Tampa companies Grant called both refused to help until the manager returned in the morning.

Reserving her a room in the local hotel was out of the question and Harley probably wouldn't agree to lodgings as far away as Tampa or Orlando. At least, not yet. He thought about hiding her with his grandmother, but how would he explain Harley to Nanna Lil?

Grant was stuck with her.

Shifting onto his right shoulder, Grant tried to force away the attendant pleasure that fact brought him. He shouldn't be enjoying this predicament. He had no right to call up her image, either slick in black leather or sweet in an oversized T-shirt, with such sensual ease. But he couldn't help himself.

Gus hadn't helped matters any with the note he'd so carefully folded and shoved at Grant before he'd left. Grant had unwrapped the note just before he'd checked Harley the first time. He'd hoped his physician brother had written down what warning signs or symptoms he should look for when he woke Harley.

Instead, he'd found a foil-wrapped condom and the phrase, "You only live once" penned in bold, block letters.

Since then, he could think of little else but making love to the woman who could so easily ruin his life.

He glanced at the clock. An hour had passed since he'd last checked on her. By 3 a.m., he'd been to her room four times, each time dreading waking her from her fitful sleep, each time anticipating her dreamy yawn, sleepy azure eyes, and groggy, "I'm fine. Go to sleep."

He threw back the covers. He'd check once more. That's all. Then he'd let her sleep. If she hadn't suffered any adverse symptoms by now, she must be well on the road to recovery.

First, he shoved the condom deep into the bottom drawer of his bedside table.

Leaving the light off in his room, he crossed through the hallway, dark except for the glow of the floodlights shining through the oculus window at the front of the house. He grabbed the doorknob to the guest room, intending to enter quietly as he had before. He'd wake her by calling her name from a safe distance, then retreat. Instead, he nearly fell forward when she yanked the door open.

"I'm not getting a lick of sleep with you waking me every hour," she complained, pushing past him, pillow tucked beneath her arm and his T-shirt reaching just below her wonderfully rounded bottom. "Last time I couldn't fall back to sleep. My brain's too busy anticipating your next 'How are you feeling?'"

Her voice mocked him, but he barely noticed. His attention focused on the sexy way she walked. Gracefully, but with her toes pointed slightly out.

"Where are you going?" The question, purely instinctual since she was obviously headed to his room, sounded much more gruff than he'd intended. Still, he wasn't ready to invite her into his bed.

His groin tightened. Okay, so he was ready. He just couldn't. Not and wake up with a clear conscience. Here was a woman who appealed to his every hidden desire, even if he didn't approve of her profession. He suspected she wouldn't shy from him as Camille had. Harley probably had a few delights of her own to share.

Still, he'd never made love to a woman who didn't know who she was. How could Harley be sure about who or what she wanted when she couldn't be sure of herself?

She stopped just before she crossed the threshold into his room. Her eyelids, weighted by something more than sleepiness, hooded her bright blue irises. Though she thrust one fist onto her hip and leaned cockily sideways, her expression betrayed a deeper emotion than anger—something more akin to desperation.

"Why couldn't you just let me sleep?"

He matched her aggressive stance with one of his own, folding his arms over his chest and trying to ignore that he wore only a pair of boxers.

"Gus said I should check on you intermittently," he defended, trying to remain distant when his instinct goaded him to take her into his arms and erase the lost look from her eyes.

"He also said I should get some rest. This way, we can both be happy."

She disappeared into his darkened bedroom, reminding him of how Gus used to find excuses to sneak into his room after they'd broken their parents' ban on creepy horror flicks. From the hall, he heard the muffled squish of her negligible weight sliding onto his motionless waterbed, the soft rustle of her legs delving into the depths of his smooth cotton sheets, the appreciative feminine sigh signaling the end of all movement.

He'd definitely gone too long without a woman. With a shrug, he followed her into the room.

She'd snuggled to the right side of the king-sized bed, the comforter pulled just beneath her breasts, her midnight-tinted hair fanning into a semicircle on the pillow. She'd closed her eyes, but hadn't had time to fall asleep.

"Harley, I think—"

"Don't think. No one's going to know but you, me and the bedbugs. This way, you can see I'm okay from just across the pillows."

She wiggled, wedging deeper into the fluffy bedclothes.

He could do this. She was tired. He was tired. They'd fall immediately to sleep. He'd have no time to *really* think about the sexiest woman he'd met in years lying prone and vulnerable in his bed. A woman who catered to men's fantasies for a living.

No problem.

Sure.

He shook his head in defeat. Even with her eyes closed, she had a determined set to her shoulders. Besides, he needed sleep. In less than three hours, he had to haul himself to work and act as if nothing unusual had occurred.

He climbed into bed, turned away from her, shut his eyes and thought about his agenda for the next day—a surefire sleep aid if ever there was one. The Board members met promptly at eight o'clock. He had a nine o'clock appointment with his biggest investor. By ten....

Before he reached the third entry in his mental appointment book, Harley's perfume, or at least the haunting remnants of her distinctive cinnamon scent, teased his nostrils like freshly baked Christmas cookies—delicious, but forbidden—meant to be saved for someone else. The additional heat of her skin warmed him beneath the sheets. She turned. Her foot brushed his leg, sparking a thrill through him that brought his senses to full attention.

"This isn't working," Harley announced quietly, voicing the very thought screaming through his brain.

"Go to sleep, Harley."

"I can't."

She turned again, and this time her smooth kneecaps connected with the sensitive skin just behind his calves. She scooted away to avoid further contact, but the damage was done.

"Gus said you needed rest."

"I'm not sleepy."

For a moment, silence reigned. She didn't move. Neither did he. Neither muscle nor sheet rustled until her whisper drifted into his ear with the force of a bullhorn.

"I feel so alone."

He remained still as a statue, though his heart hammered. Four little words triggered the timing mechanism of a powerful bomb. She had no idea how her admission touched him, right in the place he hid so well. He knew all too well what it felt like to lie in bed with someone and still feel completely and utterly isolated. Again, the instinct to take her into his arms made his muscles tighten. He couldn't afford even the most simple gesture of compassion. Touching her could lead to so much more.

Kissing. Stroking. Making love.

Grant turned over to find her lying on her side, as if she'd been staring intently at the back of his head. "I'm right here."

"I know. It's just…I still feel as if I'm by myself."

He remained quiet for a long moment, unsure of what to say. "I'd offer to hold you, but…"

He should have stayed silent longer. Her body tensed so completely he practically felt an Arctic wind blow from her side of the bed. She pulled so far from him, he imagined she might fall off the side of the bed.

"Do you really find me so appalling?"

Grant's insides curdled. Nothing could be farther from the truth. "Not at all. Just the opposite. I'm not accustomed to having such a beautiful woman in my bed."

His eyes had adjusted to the dark, and by the dim blue light of the alarm clock, he could see the forlorn look in her sleepy eyes. Though she rewarded his compliment with a tiny smile, she tucked one hand beneath her pillow, and twined the other in the sheet. Judging from the tautness of the bed linen, she clutched the covers like a shield.

"Yeah, well, I'm sorry for imposing on you. I guess you didn't really plan to have a houseguest like me, did you?"

"Sometimes the most interesting moments in life are the unplanned ones."

Her eyes widened. "Who said that? Not Grant 'banker-boy' Riordan. I haven't known you that long, but that doesn't sound like you."

He rolled over onto his back and stared at the ceiling fan as it silently stirred the cool air. "Then you already know me pretty damn well."

The comment hung between them for a moment, and Harley's sorrow for him distracted her from her own condition. The fear, confusion, and loneliness that had brought her to his bedroom sifted away. She released her death grip on the sheet and slid her fingers onto his arm.

He didn't flinch as she expected. His skin, pliant and muscled, softened beneath her touch.

"Don't." Deep and thick with unchained possibilities, his voice shook her.

She nearly removed her hand, but couldn't bear to break even this tentative connection. "There's no harm in a simple touch."

"You don't know me."

"You don't know me, either. Come to think of it…" She smoothed her hand over his shoulder, filling herself with his heat. "I don't know me. You don't know how strange that feels, and Grant…I'm scared."

After the briefest hesitation, he scooped her into his arms and pulled her close. At first, she nearly pulled away. The feel of him, so warm and powerful, overwhelmed her like a high tide's crashing waves. But she quickly grew accustomed to the sensation of his strength surrounding her. She couldn't fight the urge to snuggle against him—this stranger who took her into his home and into his bed, however reluctantly, and now sought to drive her fears away. His bare chest, sprinkled with tawny hair and smelling of sandalwood soap, anchored her while her emotions churned and swelled.

She'd admitted more than she wanted to, more than she'd planned, more than she'd acknowledged even to herself. Without memories, she had nothing but the here and now. Yet the present overflowed with uncertainty, guilt, and loneliness. If he threw her out, where would she go? What would she do?

"It's normal to be frightened, Harley. But Gus thinks you'll be better soon."

"What if I'm not?"

She could hear his heart pound, feel his spine stiffen.

"I'll see you have the help you need."

She believed him. Grant Riordan, handsome financial impresario, would arrange everything. She'd known him for less than a day, yet she recognized a power-wielder when she saw one. He probably controlled millions of other people's dollars, and they trusted him to handle their futures. Why shouldn't she then trust him to handle hers, if only for a few days? A few hours? A few moments?

"Go to sleep, Harley. You need rest."

She closed her eyes, but knew she wouldn't sleep. Though he held her protectively, she still felt alone. She had no thoughts, no memories, no one she belonged to or who belonged to her to dream about as she drifted into slumber. She needed something—someone—to fill the expanding emptiness welling inside her.

More than ever, desire for Grant surged through her. His warmth enveloped her. His heartbeat thrummed in her ears. She'd never wanted anyone more—had she? It didn't matter that she could regain her memory in the morning, or that she might have a life and a lover somewhere else.

She just wanted a kiss. Nothing more.

"Grant?" She snuggled closer.

"Don't, Harley." Desperation clung to his voice like a drowning swimmer to driftwood. "I won't take advantage of your amnesia. You don't know who you are, or what you're suggesting."

How wrong he was! Lonely and frightened, she needed more than just the warmth of his arms and the feel of his chest against her face.

"Do you always do the right thing?"

"Always."

Finite and simple, his answer defined him with poignant accuracy. She might not know much about herself, but she'd already learned that Grant Riordan did what was proper and responsible—even when he didn't want to.

"Do you enjoy being so perfect?"

"Go to sleep, Harley. You already know too much about me."

"Do I? Well, at least I know something about someone. I don't know a damn thing about me." A sob caught in her throat, and she gulped air to regain her voice. "Can you imagine what that feels like?"

He could. As unlikely as it sounded, Grant knew that same hollowness. Unwittingly, Harley had jarred open a door in his heart long ago nailed shut—long ago abandoned when he decided the void simply couldn't be filled.

He kissed her then, because he wanted to, because he knew she wanted him to.

Because kissing her was the wrong thing to do.

4

HARLEY RETURNED GRANT'S KISS, holding his cheeks with her hands. The salted moisture of her tears seeped into his mouth and reluctantly, he pulled away.

"I'm sorry, Harley. I'm out of line."

She swiped the wetness from her face. "Don't be sorry. Please. I can't stand this empty feeling." Balling her fists, she crushed them between her breasts. "It's like there's nothing in here."

Grant brushed away a tear with his thumb pad, then kissed the stain from her cheek. He took her hand in his and massaged the tight knuckles until her fingers flattened and relaxed. "You may seem empty now, but you may not in the morning. What seems right now might not appeal to you so much in the light of day."

She swallowed deeply. "I can't worry about right or wrong while I feel so lost. I can only think about what I know."

Lightly touching his cheek again with tentative fingers, Harley traced a sensuous, swirling design from the top of his temple to the tip of his chin. Auburn stubble shaded his rugged jaw. The roughness bit at her, making him real, making her gasp. This man was a stranger, yet she wanted him to soothe away an ache so deep, her soul echoed like a voice calling down a bottomless well.

"Taking me in was a big risk for you. I don't remember any specifics, but I know I've never had any man be so generous to me before. Not without wanting something in return."

He smoothed his hand down her side, heating the soft material of her T-shirt, flushing the sensitive skin beneath. "Who says I don't want something from you? It's just I don't have the right to ask."

With visible restraint, he rested his hand on her hip, stopping his descent. A muscle in his jaw twitched, as if he clenched his teeth to keep from devouring her. His thighs flexed against hers. His sex grew rigid beneath the flimsy boxers. He hadn't denied wanting her, only denied acting on his desire in deference to her condition. With just a bit more coaxing, he'd make love to her, filling her with erotic memories she could cling to when her past eluded her.

She closed her eyes, briefly, not wanting to face the night's darkness alone. Not with him so close—this man she didn't know but already cherished. "What if I offered? I trust you, Grant."

He pushed her bangs away from her eyes, curling a long strand behind her ear. Her heartbeat stammered from his simple caress. "Should you?" He placed a feathery kiss on her temple. "Don't misunderstand. I wouldn't hurt you for the world." His voice, already deep and throaty, grew raspier as he spoke. "But you don't owe me this."

She twisted sideways so her body pressed against his full length. "I know. It's not that. After tomorrow, I may never see you again."

"That bothers you?"

He sounded surprised. She wished she could explain, but without her memory, she could only rely on an indistinct impression that no man—ever—had treated her with such consideration and respect.

"Yes. Does it bother you?"

A long moment passed before he spoke. "You'll see me again."

By the sapphire glow from his clock, she searched his eyes for any sign of deception, knowing full well that seeing him once her amnesia healed would be as wise as seeking comfort for her loneliness in his bed. Still, she read nothing but honesty in his gaze—and determination—as if not keeping his promise would betray him as much as her.

"You don't have much choice, do you?" she asked. "I'll be here in the morning whether you like it or not."

His grin, followed by a yawn, dried her tears completely. "I'll like it. Now, let's get some sleep, okay? I don't know how much longer I can keep up this gallant and responsible act."

An act. *Aptly described*, she decided as his eyes drifted closed and his heartbeat, still near enough for her to hear, slowed to a normal pace. Grant Riordan worked to be responsible and upright. Despite what she guessed to be many years of practice, an untamed, hungry wolf lurked beneath his sheepish exterior. In her desperation to fill the vacancies caused by her memory loss, she'd nearly sheared his carefully woven veneer.

And she didn't regret it one bit.

She waited for him to release her and claim more space for himself on the king-sized mattress, but he didn't. She *was* feeling better and didn't necessarily *need* to cling to him all night long. Her mind didn't seem so empty, her memories so remote. For the first time since she'd awakened on his living room floor, she felt neither fearful nor alone.

She did have someone who cared about her—at least for tonight—right here in her arms.

A THICK MIST MATERIALIZED the moment Harley realized she was dreaming. The faces, sounds, memories, all disappeared beneath an impenetrable white haze. The harder she struggled to break through, the denser the fog became until she woke with a start.

Harley rubbed her eyes free of sleep, blinking against the morning light pouring through the window. Once her pupils adjusted, she checked the clock. Eight-thirty. She slipped her hand beneath her hair, relieved that the swelling at the back of her head had lessened and the pain was now just a dull ache.

From the bedside, she snatched up a note addressed to her. It read:

Harley,
   Found some of Camille's old clothes. Something should fit. There are bagels in the fridge for breakfast, and I left the coffeemaker on in case you drink the stuff. Take the keys to my truck and go shopping. If anyone asks, you're my cousin from Ohio. I'll be home early.

Grant

Paired with a hand-drawn map from his house to the nearest shopping center, car keys and four crisp one-hundred-dollar bills, the note contained nothing in the least reminiscent of the tender night they'd shared. Still, Harley's heart did a little flip-flop. He wasn't turning her out at morning's light. He wanted her to stay—at least for today. And he trusted her—enough to give her free rein in his house, the keys to his truck, and a heck of a lot more money than she'd need to buy a decent pair of jeans, T-shirt and tennis shoes.

Flipping off the covers, Harley vaguely remembered Grant waking her at dawn. He'd asked her if she remembered anything, and didn't seem disappointed when she answered "no." In fact, when he busied himself showering and dressing, all the while whistling a vaguely familiar tune, she'd tried as hard as her sleepy mind would let her to recall one thing—one fact—that might clue her into her real identity.

Until sleep had mercifully reclaimed her, she could remember nothing else but Grant holding her all night long. The remnant sensations lingered on her skin, filling her with a deceptively contented warmth. She couldn't ignore the reality that she and Grant Riordan were strangers—two people with little in common except the predicament caused by her amnesia.

Today she'd destroy even that small connection by finding out who she was. As tempting as imposing on Grant Riordan for a long, luxurious time was, she felt sure someone somewhere was looking for her. She needed to help the process along.

Harley grabbed a cup of coffee before rummaging in the dusty box marked "charitable donations." Harley decided Grant's former wife's castaways were more appropriate to wear shopping than her leather pants and bikini top. With a less conspicuous wardrobe, she'd cruise down to "the strip" the doc had mentioned the night before. Perhaps someone there knew her or could tell her how to find Moana, who must be a friend. Once she attained that knowledge, she'd piece together the life she'd so freakishly lost.

Not surprisingly, the clothes were in exquisite condition. She found a sarong-style sundress made for a taller woman, though Harley devised a way to tie it so the shape still flattered her petite body. She also found a pair of slip-on sandals only a half size bigger than her own lace-up boots. Like the dress, the sandals appeared new, as if worn only once, and maybe not even outside the house.

Once dressed, Harley grabbed the car keys and headed to the garage. Grant's "truck" was actually a luxury sport utility vehicle, painted a shade of red just dark enough to be respectable. After a moment studying the controls, she breathed a sigh of relief that she hadn't forgotten how to drive. She eased the vehicle down Grant's long driveway, stopping once to marvel at the magnificent structure where she'd spent the night.

Harley couldn't remember anything concrete about her upbringing, but she felt entirely certain her childhood never included three-story mansions, top-of-the-line vehicles and four-hundred-dollar shopping sprees. The broad columns on the house and the butter-soft leather seats in the truck magnified the differences between her and Grant. His world was a foreign planet and she was the alien.

And probably an illegal one at that.

The sooner she found her way home, the better for them both.

At the gate, she shifted the truck into park and looked unsuccessfully for a mechanism to open the eight-foot wrought iron structure. After activating the windshield wipers, the cruise control and the CD player, she stopped messing with the factory-installed gadgetry and tried the second button on the garage door opener. With a whoop to celebrate her success, she eased the car onto the road and pulled to the curb until the gate closed behind her.

That was when she noticed someone watching her.

The curtain fluttered closed almost the instant Harley caught the movement from the house across the street. Bending forward, she pretended to fiddle with the radio when the drapery pulled back again. She couldn't see much except a distinctly feminine hand and a head of white hair.

Harley shook her head. She'd hardly been out of Grant's house for two minutes before the woman had spotted her. From the length of time the hand and head remained at the window, Harley figured Grant's neighborhood must have a foolproof crime watch program. She doubted anyone or anything could cruise this exclusive lane without being noticed and duly noted by the lady across the street.

Especially not something as conspicuous as a taxi.

Harley's heartbeat accelerated and her hands shook until she grabbed the steering wheel tighter. Biting her bottom lip, she mustered the courage to put the truck in reverse and back up a few feet to the neighbor's ungated drive. If she had any luck at all, Grant's curious neighbor might just hold the first clue Harley needed to find out who she was.

GRANT STARED AT his computer screen, nearly hypnotized by NASDAQ's scrolling blue numbers. On his desk, several stacks of carefully organized customer files waited for his attention. The tiny red light on the corner of his phone blinked rapidly, as if impatient for him to return the twenty or so voice-mail messages he'd received while at lunch. The market was hot today, ripe for his financial wizardry. Clients stood to make a lot of money once he got into his groove.

All he could think about was Harley.

He had to be nuts.

With his brain still reeling from Mr. Phipps's noontime interrogation, a poorly disguised version of small talk sandwiched between bites of grilled salmon, Grant was in no shape to judge his mental soundness. He'd finally convinced his boss nothing "irregular" had happened the night before. Not that Grant hadn't yearned for someone as "irregular" as Harley to enter his life. A devilish mix of sexiness and innocence, she'd robbed him of sleep while he imagined just how a woman like her should be touched. Stroked. Kissed.

In his insanity, he relived the vision of her eyes, droopy with exhaustion, liquid with loneliness. In them, he'd witnessed a rare and honest desire—the kind that could steal a man's reason in a matter of moments. With just one glance into her sapphire irises, he'd actually believed he could renounce his entire lifestyle long enough to find some freedom in Harley's welcoming arms.

Definitely cuckoo as his grandmother's favorite clock.

After instructing his secretary to bar everyone from his office, Grant took a deep breath and dialed his phone number. As he punched in the numbers, his own voice echoed in his brain. *You'll see me again.* Throughout the night and all morning long, the promise haunted him like the steady beat of ticker tape. With Harley's lusciously warm body and sparkling eyes to influence him, he ached to keep his promise. He couldn't fathom letting this dream woman slip away without knowing her better. Much better.

But with his logic returning and the realities of his high-stress, low-fun life surrounding him from every angle, he knew that keeping Harley in his life past this afternoon could never happen.

At the fourth ring of the phone, his answering machine engaged. Perhaps she couldn't find the phone. She could be in the shower. With the machine tucked into his private study, he didn't bother leaving a message she couldn't possibly hear. He waited fifteen minutes, then tried again.

No answer.

He dialed the cellular phone in his truck, but when the call transferred to his personal voice mail, he hung up and checked his watch. With two-thirty just a few minutes away, Grant couldn't imagine why Harley hadn't answered. How long did she take to shop? Camille often shopped for days, literally, when she had a clear line of credit and the use of her father's Learjet.

Of course, Harley was nothing like Camille. She actually liked being touched. Welcomed it. Invited it.

Pulling at his collar, Grant loosened his tie and tried his home number one more time. Without prompting, a dozen possibilities for her absence flew through his mind. Maybe she'd decided to take advantage of the warm weather to relax by the pool. Maybe her memory had returned and she'd left to find Moana. Maybe she'd taken the four hundred dollars and his truck and cut out without a backward glance.

"Damn it, Harley, answer the phone!"

"Hard to do since I'm right here."

He jumped at the sound of Harley's sultry voice and slammed down the phone.

"I'm sorry, Mr. Riordan." His secretary slipped in behind Harley, clutching her wedding planner to her chest like a shield. "She said you expected her."

Not like this. His gaze fell first to her shoes—which in itself, surprised him. But then Grant had a thing for spiky black pumps. The kind with a strap encircling the ankle. The kind a woman could use to walk all over a man like him. From her heels, his perusal traveled up her legs—lean, toned legs—legs specifically made to wrap around a man's waist. Tight.

Her sheer black hose, lined in back with a naughty seam, disappeared beneath a sinfully short skirt. If her suit hadn't been a brilliant red, he might not have noticed it at all. Accessorized with black wrist gloves and a large-brimmed scarlet hat, Harley's ensemble probably looked benign to a casual observer. One who didn't know what she did for a living. One who hadn't spent the better part of the day fantasizing about her.

"Did I need an appointment?" Her grin, just shy of being shrewd, curved her dark lips. She slid her sunglasses down her nose and winked as if her appearance was simply a little private joke. Private, maybe. A joke? Grant wasn't laughing.

He was barely breathing.

"It's all right, Mandy," he said to his secretary after a generous gulp of the cold coffee he'd left in his mug. "I have been expecting to hear from Harley this morning." He threw a slightly admonishing and completely counterfeit look at Harley. "Though I did expect it to be via telephone."

"I decided to do a little…research…and I couldn't wait to meet you back at your house."

"At your house?" Mandy's blond eyebrows rose so high they vanished beneath her carefully coifed bangs.

Harley removed her sunglasses completely and extended a gloved hand. "I apologize. I was in such a hurry to talk to Grant, I didn't properly introduce myself. I'm—"

"My cousin." Grant came around his desk, fighting the urge to pull Harley away from Mandy as if a touch would reveal their sham. "From Ohio. Amanda Drexler, may I introduce my cousin, Harley. Monroe. My mother's side. She's staying with me a few days."

Relief washed the paleness from Mandy's face and she shook Harley's hand enthusiastically. "Nice to meet you, Miss Monroe. I didn't know Grant—Mr. Riordan—had any cousins. Are you first cousins? Second?"

Harley answered for him. "Third, actually. Twice removed."

The addition, so offhanded, added credence to Grant's lie in a way that made him marvel. Her head injury hadn't slowed her mental reflexes in the least. He wondered why someone so quick-witted and resourceful would choose stripping as a profession.

"Nice to meet you, Ms. Drexler. I didn't know Grant had such a lovely secretary."

Harley's backward glance seemed to ask, "No scandals, right?" but her grin at Mandy proved convincing and his secretary's smile calmed the rapid beating in his chest. Though well-meaning and loyal, Mandy had been distracted for the last few weeks preceding her wedding. Tomorrow she would marry Steve, Grant's guest of honor at last night's gathering. The wrong innocent remark could initiate a tidal wave of trouble. Steve and Grant had been friends since childhood. Steve knew damned well Grant didn't have any cousins in the whole United States, much less in Ohio.

Of course, Steve also knew Harley was a stripper—if he didn't have his own case of memory loss from the amount of beer he'd consumed the night before. Grant doubted this blushing bride-to-be would be so gracious if she'd seen her intended pawing Harley last night. In her ignorance, Mandy beamed as if she'd discovered some delicious secret.

"Please, call me Mandy. How long are you here for?"

Harley stepped toward Grant. A scent, vaguely familiar and clearly erotic, drifted from her skin. Only after inhaling deeply did he recognize the fragrance. His cologne. Mixed with Harley. The result sent him stalking back to his desk. He tore open the first envelope in a stack of mail and pretended to return to his work.

Harley followed him across the room at an unhurried pace. "Never can tell. This trip wasn't, to say the least, planned very well." When she leaned on his desk, her suit jacket folded open just enough for him to glimpse a scrap of black lace.

Madness stirred.

"Thank you, Mandy," Grant interrupted, tossing the unread letter aside. "I can manage for the rest of the afternoon." He glanced at his watch. "You should have been out of here two hours ago."

"I didn't want to leave until Mr. Phipps left your office. I haven't been with the firm that long," she explained to Harley. "With our honeymoon and everything…"

"You're the one getting married tomorrow?" Harley asked.

Mandy's toothy smile stretched even farther across her face. "I can hardly believe it myself." Mandy backed toward the door. "Mother's expecting me at the salon in an hour. We'll see you at six, Grant?"

"St. Bartholemew's. Six sharp."

"The rehearsal dinner will be right after, at Don Gianni's. Oh, Miss Monroe, Steve and I would just love for you to come. You could meet Grant's friends and keep him company. I've been trying for months to convince him to bring a date for the wedding. You are *third* cousins, right? Hardly related at all."

Grant's lungs stopped pumping air. No, they weren't related, but that wasn't the reason he had to keep his distance. Harley drove him crazy. Her eyes quickened his pulse. Her voice turned his insides to hot lava. Even now, standing in his office with his secretary only a few feet away, he could feel the pressure of his swelling sex against his zipper. If he were another man, he'd order Mandy to go to her appointment immediately so he could lock the door and make love to Harley on his imported leather couch.

But Grant wasn't another man. He had a reputation to protect. Responsibilities to his firm. To his grandmother. Harley, on the other hand, was a dream—a tangible illusion he could never maintain in his world. Strippers, even classy ones, didn't easily blend into the conservative enclave he currently called home. At least, not for long. People like Wilhelmina Langley and Howell Phipps had ways to root out a stranger's deepest, darkest secrets.

He desperately sought some foolproof excuse to deny Mandy's invitation, but he came up blank. He couldn't afford another foray into fantasy. Neither could she. How could they spend an entire evening lying to his friends, especially when the guys all knew the truth?

He nearly choked when he saw how Mandy's invitation lit Harley's face.

"How could someone say no to an offer like that?"

5

"REALLY," HARLEY CONTINUED, oblivious to the gagging sound that erupted from the back of Grant's throat. "It's so sweet of you to think about someone else right before your big day." Harley took Mandy's hand again and patted it with a warmth that seemed older than the both of them combined. "I have plans tonight with an old friend who lives nearby. Your invitation's so considerate, I hate declining."

Mandy frowned in disappointment. "I understand."

Last night in his kitchen, Grant would have bet his entire lost fortune that Harley hadn't the capacity to be dishonest. Yet in potentially explosive situations, she made a convincing actress.

Mandy had already opened the door to exit when she turned. "But Grant, I'm sure you'd like your cousin to meet your friends some other time."

"Of course. Next time she visits."

"Why wait that long? What about tomorrow at the wedding? It's only a couple of hours in the evening and you can leave the reception any time you like. You want her to come with you, don't you, Grant? To keep you company?"

Grant wasn't as adept at acting as Harley. He couldn't see Harley's face, but he knew from the passing seconds of silence that she had no intention of fielding this question for him. The truth was, if Steve hadn't asked him to be the best man and Mandy hadn't been the finest secretary he'd ever had, he would have found an ironclad excuse not to attend the ceremony. Weddings reminded him of Camille and Camille reminded him of his ulcer. Of course, with Harley to distract him, the whole ordeal just might be tolerable.

What the hell, he thought. *If she's going to drive me crazy, I might as well enjoy the ride.*

"Mandy, I've learned it's not wise to argue with a nervous bride. I'd love Harley to come with me."

Mandy clapped her hands together triumphantly. "It's settled then. I'll make a few quick changes to the seating arrangements and we're all set. I'm so glad Grant won't be alone on what promises to be the most romantic night of the year!"

Before he could remind his matchmaking secretary that Harley was his cousin, supposedly anyway, she'd bounded from the room and closed the door behind her. Harley extracted a pin from her hair and removed her hat, sailing it across his desk like a Frisbee.

"I'd bet big money Mandy used to be a cheerleader."

Grant lifted the broad-brimmed hat from its landing spot on the day's stock reports. "University of Florida. All four years."

"I like her." Harley tugged at her gloved index finger. "She obviously thinks a lot of you, to care about your personal life like she does."

With undivided attention, Grant watched Harley struggle with the glove. When she used her teeth to loosen the snug material, his mouth dried. She had such perfect lips. Curved. Silken. Beneath her lipstick lived a soft blush color that would likely darken to a rich shade of pink when he kissed her.

He cleared his throat. "Mandy's a good person."

Harley slid the glove from her hand, revealing nails sleek with a crimson coat of glossy color. The women he knew would never dare wear such a shade. Not unless they meant to draw attention to some new bauble they'd recently acquired. But Harley didn't need jewelry to attract his attention to her hands. The memory of her soft palms cupping his stubble-rough cheeks still lingered, along with the tortuous warmth of her fingers curled against his chest.

He was a goner.

She'd pinned her hair away from her face, but her layered style left wisps fringing her face, drawing attention to her liquid sapphire eyes. And though she'd probably meant the suit to be conservative, more than just the color made the outfit nearly as sexy as her leather pants and jacket. The cut emphasized her firm breasts, tapered waist and God help him, her magnificent legs. Harley wasn't tall—her legs weren't long—but with curses to the madman who invented pantyhose, Grant couldn't resist fantasizing about guiding those legs around his hips while he took her on the ride of her life.

"Regretting it already?"

He snapped from his revelry with an unattractive snort.

"Excuse me?"

"That expression on your face." She removed the other glove and tucked them in her tiny purse. "I'm assuming you're regretting giving in to Mandy. It's okay if you want me to back out. My going to the wedding is a big risk. What if someone recognizes me?"

Leaning sideways, Harley propped her hip on his desk and looked at him expectantly. "Grant?"

He wanted to tell her how beautiful, how utterly sexy she was, but he couldn't afford the luxury. Despite his own desires, he and Harley needed to concentrate on her amnesia. On finding her friend Moana. On unlocking her past.

On keeping him from ravishing her on his desk.

He slid his letter opener into a manila envelope and sliced sideways with a vengeance. "Mandy wasn't about to take no for an answer. We'll just have to play it by ear."

Harley glanced away. "Sounds like a plan."

The brief glimpse of disappointment he thought he saw disappeared when she snapped open her purse and pulled out a scrap of paper.

"Here."

Grant looked down at the company name, Sunshine Cab, and the Tampa address. "What's this?"

"Our first clue. I coerced the dispatcher into telling me that a driver named Hank dropped me off last night."

"So you did more this morning than blow my money on that outfit?"

"A heck of a lot more." She slipped her hand back in her purse and tossed over two hundred and fifty dollars and change onto his desk.

He quickly tallied the damage. "You got that get-up for less than two hundred bucks?" Her clothes might have been sexy, but they didn't look cheap.

"I wouldn't have if I'd shopped where you sent me. Mrs. Langley told me about this consignment shop on Grove Street. I bought this outfit, a pair of jeans, several pairs of shorts and tops, three pairs of shoes, some makeup and an adorable mini dress. I thought the clothes would last a few days, but I didn't count on being invited to a wedding…"

Harley's explanation had died away in his mind the minute the name "Mrs. Langley" registered in his brain. Actually, he'd heard her speak, but the words failed to make sense.

"Who?"

Her eyes widened. "Mandy, your secretary. Remember, she invited me to the wedding tomorrow? I'll need something to wear. She's already seen this and I..."

"No, I mean, who sent you to the consignment shop?"

Harley's perplexed look made his heart stammer. Hadn't he mentioned that she should stay clear of his neighbor? Hadn't he warned her that of all people in the entire town of Citrus Hill, Mrs. Wilhelmina Langley was the last person who should learn that Grant had a beautiful woman staying in the First Investment corporate mansion?

Hadn't he written DO NOT TALK TO THE TERMINATOR ACROSS THE STREET in bold black letters across the top of the note he'd left?

"Mrs. Langley. That sweet woman that lives across the street from you."

Obviously not.

"Oh, Lord."

As if falling from the top of a high-rise, Grant let a downward pull plop him into his chair. Not only was Wilhelmina Langley hell-bent on finding another First Investment sex scandal to break in her column, the woman could detect a lie with accuracy well beyond current technology. Even Harley's impressively casual style of twisting the truth wouldn't fool her.

The jig was up.

"Grant? You look pale. Do you want some water?"

"Only if it has a fifth of Scotch in it."

"Excuse me?"

"Wilhelmina Langley knows you're staying with me?"

"Of course. I think that's why she seemed so anxious to help me. The minute she found out I was staying with you, she invited me in for lemonade and we had a nice little chat."

A burst of pain exploded in Grant's stomach. "A little chat."

"What are you so uptight about? I told her the cousin story and she bought it hook, line and sinker. She's the one I got the cab company name from. She saw the cab parked in front of your gate last night."

"And she saw you get out in your trench coat, despite the fact that the temperature was nearly eighty degrees?"

Harley's lips twisted as if he'd asked the most inane question ever conceived. "If she did, she didn't mention it."

Of course not. She'll keep that tiny detail as food for conjecture in her next column.

"I'm as good as fired."

Harley stood. "What are you talking about? Mrs. Langley said nothing but good things about you. And she couldn't wait to help me. I told her I left a bag in the cab that dropped me off, but I couldn't remember the name of the company. She gave me the name and directions to a reasonably priced store where I could shop until I found my luggage. Would she have done all that if she wanted to hurt you?"

"Just a means to an end."

Harley rolled her eyes. "You're paranoid. Without my memory, I'm very in tune with other people. Mrs. Langley sincerely wanted to help me."

"It doesn't matter now. Her column doesn't hit the paper until Sunday. That gives us two days to find out who you are and find me another line of work."

"Well, Mr. Gloom and Doom, I suggest you try detective work."

"Detective work?"

"You can learn from me. So far, I'm pretty darned good." She snatched the slip of paper with the cab company's name and address from his hand. "I spoke to Hank, the driver, after leaving Mrs. Langley's house, which is why I was so excited I came straight here. After shopping, of course."

"Of course. This Hank remembered you?"

"Seems I'm unforgettable."

Grant couldn't argue the point.

"He picked me up at a restaurant called the Village Inn on Dale Mabry Highway. He said there are several strip clubs in the neighborhood. It's not much, but it's a place to start. I could check out some of these clubs while you go to your rehearsal and dinner."

Ordinarily, Grant would never contemplate setting foot in an exotic dance club. If a client, or worse, a Board member, caught wind of Grant's attendance, he'd be canned in a heartbeat. Thanks to Harley's innocent tête-à-tête with Mrs. Langley, that outcome was just as good as written in stone anyway.

He had nothing to lose. Besides, the idea of retreating into a forbidden world of sex and sin with Harley as his guide tempted the hungriest part of him more than he could resist.

"I don't want you to go alone. I'll take you after the dinner."

Last night, he'd held back from Harley because of her condition. His conscience, although weakened by his overpowering attraction, held him fast to the conviction that he couldn't explore his passion with her until she knew who she was. Tonight, that could change.

Harley's smile reinforced his decision to throw caution to the wind. "You'd do that for me? You've already done so much."

And once she regained her memory, he intended to do much, much more.

"Yeah, well, I'm just one heck of a guy. A heck of an unemployed guy, but that's a moot point."

Harley clucked her tongue as she replaced her hat with a jaunty tilt. "If you're so worried, I'll stop by Mrs. Langley's on the way back and make sure—"

"No." The word exploded from his lips so loudly, Harley stabbed herself with her hat pin. She impaled him just as sharply with a threatening squint.

"Sorry." He adjusted his position in his chair. "Just stay away from that woman from this minute on. Far away."

Harley crossed her arms beneath her breasts, emphasizing the perfect shape of her cleavage. "Why does she spook you so much? She seems like a charming, although lonely, lady who lives on a street where she cares about her neighbors."

"Cares enough to ruin their careers."

She leaned against his desk again, this time careful to push aside his reports. "I don't think I like you very much when you're maligning sweet elderly women."

"Ha!" Her comment gave him reason to scoot his chair back, away from that tempting scent lingering on her skin. "That battle-ax is as sweet as a rancid peanut. Just ask my two predecessors."

Harley pulled the keys to his truck from her tiny purse, suddenly anxious to put some distance between her and Grant. "She told me about that."

"Did she show you the skulls and crossbones she's carved into her computer?"

"She showed me the articles. I read them." Wilhelmina Langley had a particular talent for description that no doubt filled the citizens of conservative Citrus Hill with self-righteous rage. Without being graphic, the carefully crafted words suggested the details of sordid sexual escapades with the power of a porno flick. "Seems both those perverts got what they deserved."

Grant pursed his lips, and Harley stifled a grin. Making Grant Riordan concede a point, even the smallest one, seemed a Herculean task—though she wasn't quite sure why. So far, he'd been more than gracious, accommodating even, to her, despite her potential danger to his career. She'd read the venom Wilhelmina Langley could spit in her column, and Grant was smart to steer clear of trouble with this woman watching his every move. But speaking with his neighbor, sharing a homemade glass of lemonade in the comfort of her parlor, clued Harley that Mrs. Langley didn't wield her weapon haphazardly. She hunted shysters and scam artists, not hardworking, kindhearted executives like Grant.

Of course, Grant was harboring a stripper in the corporate mansion and pretending she was his long-lost cousin from Ohio. To a curious eye, especially one attuned to scandal, the situation wouldn't appear very innocent.

Boy, have I screwed up.

Grant shoved some files into his top desk drawer. "Those perverts might have deserved to lose their jobs, but the exposure of the articles ruined them. There are ways to deal with irresponsible managers without subjecting their families and friends to humiliation."

This time, Harley had to surrender. "I see your point. I'll keep a wide berth from Mrs. Langley on the way back. I don't want to cause you trouble."

Her teasing grin cracked the stoic expression Grant wore. "As Gus said last night, no trouble at all. How are you feeling anyway?" His tone softened, along with the rigid lines around his eyes and mouth. "You look…healthy."

Suddenly, her suit seemed a tad stifling. "My headache disappeared the minute I got the cab company name. Maybe my memory will return by tonight and you won't have to worry about me blowing your reputation with Mrs. Langley."

Grant stood, inching toward her as he reached for a stack of files behind her. "You are pretty…convincing. Maybe ole Wilhelmina *did* buy your story."

She shrugged, trying to ignore the increased tempo her heart beat when Grant leaned even closer. The scent of his cologne, so much richer and muskier than the aroma she'd spritzed on herself this morning, permeated the air around her like an intoxicating cloud.

She couldn't resist inhaling deeply before she spoke. "I won't take any more chances."

"That's a good girl." The whisper, spoken so close to her ear, singed the tiny hairs that had fallen loose from her French twist and sent a sensation like melted chocolate oozing through her veins. The warmth snaked around her nape, nearly choking her with unhampered desire.

She sure didn't feel much like a good girl with Grant so near. Her mind jumbled with images of desk tops and sweaty bodies. Flying clothes. Scattering papers. Groping hands and long, sensual kisses.

Had to be Langley's article. Reading about illicit sex undoubtedly primed her for such aberrant thoughts.

Aberrant, but delicious.

She took two steps toward the door, fighting the urge to gasp. "I'm sure you have work to do."

He only nodded, but his hesitant movement and intense stare implied much more. Had a similarly indiscreet image popped into his head as well? Was that why he'd stood so near his hot breath had practically made love to her neck?

Three more steps and she'd nearly reached the door. The hot haze clouding her mind drifted away, allowing her to remember the message she'd meant to give him.

"Oh, by the way, your grandmother called."

"Nanna Lil?" His hand was already on his phone's receiver, his finger pressing the speed-dial before Harley had a chance to respond. "Did you speak to her? Is she okay?"

"I heard her over your machine. She just said to call when you get home, but since you'll be late…"

Grant held his hand up and spoke into the phone. "Mrs. Blake? Grant, here. Could I speak to Lil?"

He covered the mouthpiece with his hand while he waited. "She fell last year. Has trouble getting around. Mrs. Blake's her private nurse."

That explained the pile of contractor's bills stacked on Grant's desk in his home office. Wheelchair ramps, handrails and adjusted countertops didn't come cheap. She hadn't meant to snoop, but she'd been looking for a phone book and the number to the cab company. He was obviously bankrolling the entire renovation to his grandmother's home, noted on one bill as "1920's Victorian-styled."

"Hey, Nanna. It's Grant." His grin bloomed so bright, she nearly pulled out her sunglasses. She'd never seen anyone so completely and openly happy. His little-boy expression prompted a smile of her own. "No, I'm still at the office. I just checked my messages."

She raised her eyebrows at his white lie. He shrugged in response. His grin never faltered.

"Yes, I'll be there Sunday. You tell Mr. Ross not to adjust those rails until I inspect the work myself. I'd come sooner, but—"

His grandmother obviously cut him off as he fell deferentially silent. "Yes, ma'am. I'll tell Mandy and Steve you said so. I'll call you tomorrow." Another pause. "Okay, I'll see you Sunday then."

He hung up the phone, but the youthful joy in his expression lasted for the few silent moments hanging between them.

"Are you doing construction?" Harley asked, afraid her lack of curiosity might alert him to her spying.

His smile disappeared. "Lil's lived in that house all her life. She was born there only a year after my great-grandfather finished it. But it's old and not wheelchair-friendly. I'm trying to fix that."

"All alone? Doesn't Gus help?"

"When he can. He's got a lot of debt from medical school he's still paying off."

Harley nodded and dropped the subject, not wanting to prolong the melancholy suddenly shading his features. "She's lucky to have you."

A semblance of a smile returned. "I'm the lucky one. I only see my parents once a year, maybe twice if they're not traveling during Christmas break. Gus and Lil are really the only family I have. Lil's a grand old dame, too. Southern, proud, educated. You'd like her. She'd like you."

"Not if she found out what I do for a living."

His gaze once again darkened with the shadow she recognized as desire. "Harley, you are a very alluring and charming woman."

The momentary break from his magnetism ceased.

His voice deepened. His grin turned hypnotic. The considerable space between them suddenly resembled mere inches.

Clearing her throat, Harley clutched the doorknob. "Are you coming back to the house before your dinner?"

Grant tugged at his tie. "I don't think so. I have a ton of work to finish. I should be home around nine or so. Then we'll head for Tampa."

She left with a tiny wave. The minute she shut the door behind her, the atmosphere around her lightened as if imbued with pure helium. She scurried through Grant's reception area, thankful for Mandy's absence and the powerful air-conditioning on the second floor.

As she opened the glass door to the lobby, she kept her gaze to the floor. She didn't need a mirror to know how feverish and uncousinly her face looked after just a few minutes alone with Grant. Or how much she was in desperate need of a frigid shower.

A warm blast of humid air hit her as she exited the building. Smack in the center of Citrus Hill's small but bustling downtown, the First Investment building loomed like a monarch over the antique shops, boutiques and jewelry stores that took up retail space on either side. City Hall, just a half block down, seemed small in comparison to Grant's company's imposing Colonial.

The effect was more than symbolic.

After reading Mrs. Langley's articles and visiting Grant's office, Harley knew just how important Grant's job was to the community. And to him. Amid the invoices for the renovations, she'd also found a letter from Grant's ex-wife's attorney. Grant commanded millions, but he had huge bills. If he lost his job because of her, she'd never forgive herself.

On the way to where she'd parked, she crossed in front of a golf shop and caught her reflection in the plate glass window. Who was she trying to fool most, herself? She didn't belong in designer clothes. She didn't belong in a luxury vehicle. Mostly, she didn't belong in Grant's house where her presence alone threatened his livelihood.

She hurried to the truck, got in and pulled away from the curb with her gaze trained on the road. No matter what she and Grant did or didn't find out tonight, she couldn't risk staying at his house past tomorrow morning. Grant didn't need a woman like her in his life. He needed someone classy—reserved, appropriate—someone who could visit him at his office without entertaining fantasies of making love to him on his desk. Someone who'd only taken her clothes off for a man she loved.

HESITANTLY, GRANT SLID his key into the side door lock. Through the sheers on the door's half window, he could see Harley at the kitchen table, absently flipping through a magazine, her bare feet propped on the chair across from her.

With careless interest, she perused the articles, pausing to read a line or two, frowning in obvious disagreement, nodding when something suited her. When she leaned forward, her breasts pressed against the slick tile tabletop, making her appear rounder and fuller in her tight, striped T-shirt. While she read, she balanced the tip of her left pinkie nail on the edge of her bottom teeth—never biting down, but drawing his complete interest to those incredibly luscious lips of hers.

She's sexy just turning pages.

He'd never met anyone like her. Not really. Women with Harley's freedom of spirit couldn't exist in his world—at least, not for long. Rigid rules of decorum and expectations of perfection killed all spontaneity and daring. When he'd met his ex-wife in college, he'd caught a glimpse of such independence in Camille. But after the wedding and his acceptance of a position in her father's firm, Camille molded herself into the perfect executive's wife. By the time he'd made his first million, their marriage had become a passionless sham. His attempts to rekindle what he now admitted was a lackluster love life only hastened and embittered their separation.

He'd quickly realized that the kind of woman he needed and the kind he wanted were worlds apart. His fantasy lover could silence a trading floor just by smiling. Could reinvigorate him after a losing day with a sultry glance. Unfortunately, women like that didn't come along often. He'd given up looking and settled for thrills of the financial sort, especially after Camille milked him dry in the divorce. He hadn't regretted his choice—until Harley.

She renewed his abandoned desires. Made him ache in places he'd forgotten existed.

And it felt great.

He had no idea how he'd survive visiting strip clubs with her. She made his kitchen erotic. He suddenly had a very naughty thought involving a spatula and orange blossom honey. With her blatant sexuality, enhanced by such iniquitous surroundings as nude dance joints, he'd undoubtedly fall even farther toward utter dereliction of his long-held standards of behavior.

He couldn't wait to go.

With an enthusiastic twist, he opened the door. "Honey, I'm home."

Harley flipped the copy of *Money* magazine closed

and crossed her feet at the ankles. "I bet you say that to all the amnesiac strippers who stay at your mansion."

"It's a regular catch phrase." He froze just inside the threshold as she slid her slim legs off the chair and tucked them beneath her, causing her black mini skirt to ride up high on her smooth, tanned thighs. Before she caught him staring, he headed toward her with a Styrofoam box filled with manicotti from Don Gianni's. "I brought you dinner. My cupboards are usually pretty bare."

Harley opened the container and inhaled. Closing her eyes, she shimmied her shoulders and smiled when the scent proved aromatically enticing. "Mmm. Smells delicious. But I'll have to save it for later." She refolded the top reluctantly. "I told you I'd make a great detective. I managed to hunt out a meal from your measly pantry. Who does your grocery shopping, Kate Moss?"

Grant had to stop and think. He knew Kate Moss wasn't the answer, but he truly had no real idea how staple items such as milk, bread, pastas and chips reached the bare confines of his refrigerator and pantry. Since he'd moved into the corporate mansion, the food appeared on a seemingly regular basis—enough to keep him satisfied during a rare case of the munchies. He didn't eat at home often, opting instead for restaurant dinners with Gus or clients or home-cooked meals at Nanna Lil's. "I suppose the housekeeper sees to the food. I'm not home much. It's probably part of her job description."

"Didn't you hire her?"

"She came with the house. I don't spend a great deal of time here."

Harley swiveled toward him, her black hair brushing against her shoulders and caressing her cheek. Her serious frown didn't keep her from looking thoroughly kissable. "I don't see why you would. Is any of this furniture actually yours? This room isn't so bad, I guess, but the rest seems so…corporate."

The word spilled from her lips with utter distaste. He slid his keys onto the butcher block island in the center of the room and shrugged out of his jacket. "Corporate? I don't remember seeing that style profiled in the last issue of *Architectural Digest*."

"You know what I mean. Well decorated, down to the fine porcelain and corded throw pillows. But there's nothing personal anywhere. No pictures of your brother, memorabilia from college, no silly gift some well-meaning client gave you that doesn't really match anything, but you don't have the heart to throw away."

So, she'd searched the house before settling in the kitchen in her minuscule skirt and adorable shoeless feet. But she hadn't looked for valuables. Those were in plain sight, on careful display for clients or competitors he might have over for drinks before a high-powered dinner.

Harley looked for him in the furnishings. She'd embarked on a quest for treasures of the insightful kind. Not surprisingly, she found nothing of use.

"I have trinkets and memorabilia." He carefully folded his jacket over a chair back. "Just not here. They don't really belong. The house is owned by the corporation, not by me."

Standing, Harley slid her hands into the front pockets of her skirt and stretched her ankles, extending her height an inch or so. She cocked her head slightly and stared at him with her remarkably blue eyes. "And you don't want to be just like the house. Owned by the corporation, I mean."

He shook his head and laughed quietly. "Are you sure you are a stripper?" He backed away and busied himself by filling a glass with ice and water. "I'd invest big money you're actually a psychiatrist. Maybe doing some unorthodox research project exploring male sexual fantasies. You masquerade as a stripper for a few nights—" he took a sip of the cold liquid before setting his glass on the counter "—for firsthand experience."

She rocked back on her heels. "I don't think so. But I have been meaning to ask you about that."

He mirrored her stance, digging his hands into his own pockets, hoping to hide the hardening he suffered from so regularly with Harley around. "About male sexual fantasies?"

She paused to consider her answer, and Grant felt the stir quickening in his groin.

"No."

She was probably better off. Definitely better off. At that moment, Grant could create a picture of male sexual fantasies that would send the most staid psychoanalyst sprinting toward an industrial-strength freezer.

She slid her fingers into her hair, hooking the ebony strands behind her ear. A delectable ear. An ear he could spend the next few hours nibbling.

"Did I say anything before you pummeled me with that book?"

He drained the rest of his glass in one gulp. "I didn't pummel you with the book." He slipped past her, grabbed the manicotti and put it in the refrigerator. "You backed up to avoid Steve's groping and bumped into the bookshelf."

"Steve was groping me?"

"Attempting to. He was drunk and his aim was off."

"Where were you?"

In a bright flash, Harley saw Grant rushing toward her, panic and passion darkening his eyes. He was leaping, airborne, with such determination, she'd stepped back to avoid being consumed. Yet like her dream this morning, the image sped away the moment she realized what it was.

A memory.

"Harley?"

Grant placed his hand beneath her elbow, and she realized she'd nearly fallen backward.

"I just saw you," she said.

"I'm right here."

"Last night. Before the accident."

His grip tightened. "You remembered something?"

I remembered you wanted me. Brief but powerful, the recollection revealed an intense sensation of passion and need. Mutual need. When he'd shot toward her, she'd retreated, not out of fear of him, but of herself. She'd wanted him too.

"You're sure we didn't know each other before last night?" she asked, desperate to make sense of the disturbing impression. If they'd been strangers, how could she have had such an overwhelming desire for him? A desire that remained even when her memory did not.

"Positive. Harley, what did you remember?"

She couldn't tell him. Such a revelation would bring them no closer to learning her identity. She'd only embarrass herself more than she had already. She was a stripper, for goodness' sake. A romantic relationship with her, even a brief one, could devastate his career.

"I remembered the book. Falling. Hitting me. For an instant, I saw you running toward me. Nothing that helps."

Grant placed his other hand on her shoulder, and for

a moment, she hoped he might take her into his arms. Instead, the muscles and joints in his arms locked, keeping her at a safe distance.

Right where she should be.

"I spoke to Gus at the rehearsal. He did some research and thinks the amnesia wasn't caused by the bump on the head exactly, but is your brain's way of protecting you from some traumatic event. In cases such as yours, the memory returns in bits and pieces. This is a start." He didn't try to disguise the excitement in his voice. "If we find Moana tonight, maybe she'll trigger something else. You could regain your memory before the night is over."

She nodded and forced herself to smile, acting as if she shared his enthusiasm. She should have. She knew she should. She'd already decided she had to leave Grant's house as soon as possible. Leaving, after all, was the right thing to do.

So why couldn't she bring herself to do it?

6

HARLEY TOOK A DEEP BREATH when Grant turned away from the burly man at the club door and walked back toward her. They'd visited three nude dance establishments in the last hour, and after encountering a rowdy group of college boys in the parking lot of the first, Grant insisted she wait in the car. If anyone at the club knew Moana, or a stripper named Harley, he'd signal.

Like a coward, she'd agreed. Grant's forceful use of cool logic and blatant intimidation proved impossible to fight, particularly when she still reeled from his sudden enthusiasm for finding out her real identity. He'd probably rethought his decision to escort her to such a public event as tomorrow's wedding, particularly after her bumbling with his nosy neighbor. Although she'd already decided her leaving would be best, his eager attitude stuck in her craw.

So what if they hailed from different ends of the universe. So what if they had nothing in common except a phenomenally strong physical attraction. So what if she'd been the one to climb, uninvited, into his bed and practically beg him to kiss away her loneliness. She didn't want to be just a brief encounter he'd laugh about later. She wanted to know him better, discover more about the untamed man he hid beneath his staid facade. The promise of such intense loving intrigued her, tempted her to the point of near obsession.

Yet from the triumphant look in Grant's eyes as he

tapped on the passenger door window, she doubted she'd be around long enough to learn his favorite color.

And that was probably best.

She pressed the button that rolled down the window.

"The bouncer knows Moana, but hasn't seen her for over a month. Supposedly, she took a job at a club on the causeway, but he heard she's not there anymore either."

"Does he know me?"

"No, but there's another dancer inside named Joy who keeps in touch with Moana. She's about to go on, so we need to hurry. I slipped him a fifty to let us in the back entrance."

Harley rolled up the window without a word and allowed Grant to open the door.

"You don't have to go in. I can ask Joy about Moana for you. If you're uncomfortable."

Harley snatched her tiny red purse—the four-dollar bargain from the consignment shop—and swung it over her shoulder, nearly knocking Grant in the face. She slammed the door and stalked silently down the side alley, not waiting for Grant to set the alarm.

"Why should I be uncomfortable?" she said once she heard him fall in step behind her. "I've probably worked in worse places than this."

In truth, an icy shiver hovered just below Harley's spine, ready to shimmy straight up the minute she stepped through the black steel door at the end of the alley. Flashing with neon and packed with cars, this club wasn't the worst they'd visited tonight. And far from the best. The air surrounding the single-storied concrete block structure reeked of tobacco. Though no alcohol was allowed inside, the dizzying smells of stale beer, pungent whiskey and raw vomit assailed her as she scurried alongside the moldy wall. She nearly gagged when her shoes made a sucking noise as she climbed the single step.

"Harley, slow down."

Grant grabbed her arm as she reached for the doorknob. She tried to ignore the strength of his grip, the warmth of his palm against her bare skin, the soothing command in his deep voice. This man didn't want her around. Didn't need her around. She could destroy him just by being in his presence. She couldn't afford to let herself fantasize any longer.

"Slow down? You should be anxious to get rid of me."

Calmly, he turned her to face him. "I'm anxious for you to regain your memory. Aren't you?"

She'd been asking herself the same question all afternoon. After Grant dispelled the overwhelming fear of the unknown she'd experienced the night before, she'd felt safe enough to begin exploring what might be a disturbing past.

Yet the eagerness with which she'd pursued the cabdriver this afternoon vanished the minute Grant seemed excited to see her go. Her net of security dropped away. She no longer wanted to know how often she'd been employed at rat holes like this one, or what downward turn her life had taken to lead her to stripping in the first place. If not for the nagging suspicion that someone waited for her somewhere, she might have given in to the temptation to start her life over again with a fresh slate.

Maybe with Grant.

Except he didn't want her.

She glanced aside, avoiding his assessing gaze. "I want to know if anyone misses me. If I belong anywhere or with anyone."

He caressed her elbow with gentle friction. "Then here's the best place to start."

Again, Harley wondered why she clung so tightly to this reluctant man she barely knew. She glanced over her shoulder at the massive rusting door and found her answer. Grant was everything her life more than likely was not—ordered, respectable, controlled. Perhaps her mind did *choose* to shut off the minute she'd seen him hurdling across the room toward her, as if intending to rescue her from some horrid fate.

She dug her heel into the ground and swung around with renewed vigor. She could damn well rescue herself, thank you.

"Let's do it."

As PROMISED, the bouncer's partner, Carl, admitted Grant and Harley after two solid knocks on the door. The entire backstage area pounded with bone-jarring bass and reverberated with the whoops and hollers of the male patrons out front. Behind the scenes, the dancers, clad in satiny costumes of various sizes and degrees of suggestiveness, shouted to each other over the din, checked their hair in lighted mirrors, puffed on cigarettes and sipped bottled water. Only after Carl directed them into a neat, contemporary-style office could Grant bring his attention back to the matter at hand.

He directed Harley toward a sleek leather chair and positioned himself behind her. Moments later, the door reopened and a dancer entered wearing a classically tailored gold-sequined dress. Long-sleeved and high-necked, the costume looked nothing like what Grant had imagined. She seemed dressed for an evening at the opera rather than stripping. Only when she turned around to close the door behind her and he saw the low-slung, backless design did he know this was the woman they sought.

She cut to the chase as soon as she braced her hands on the chair behind the cluttered desk. Her dark hair, pulled up into a loose tumble atop her head, hung around her face and eyes like black fringe. "Sal said you were asking questions about Moana."

"Do you know her?" Harley asked, her tone both determined and nonthreatening. She'd acted pensive and moody since he'd returned from the rehearsal dinner. He didn't know what to expect from her now. Then again, he never knew what to expect from Harley.

Which, of course, made him desire her all the more.

"The answer is going to depend." Joy swung the chair around and settled herself in with grace—the same grace Harley displayed—the grace of a dancer. Fair-skinned and brunette, she nearly mirrored Harley. Same look, same age, yet taller and definitely more jaded. Joy's eyes, dark and wary, possessed none of the naive wonder Grant often caught in Harley's baby blues.

Joy knew the score. And she probably had a price.

He pulled out his wallet and offered her a crisp fifty. "Will this do?"

Joy waved the cash away. "Save your money for my next set. I want to know *exactly* why you're looking for Moana before I say another word. Don't even think about strong-arming me, big boy. Carl is waiting just outside the door."

Harley slipped her hand over her mouth, undoubtedly amused anyone would think Grant capable of strong-arming anyone. Not that he didn't have the bulk or the skill. He just preferred more civilized forms of persuasion.

In this case, however, the truth would serve just fine.

He swung around Harley's chair and took the seat beside her. "Moana was hired to perform at a bachelor party at my home last night. She didn't show."

"Did you pay her in advance and come here trying to collect?"

"I went in her place," Harley provided, her voice suddenly small.

"You strip?" Joy's assessing stare tallied Harley from head to toe. "I've never seen you before."

Harley straightened her shoulders and leaned forward. "Do you know Moana well?"

Joy eased back into the chair. "About as well as we ladies can. We met at a tanning salon about two years ago and danced at the same clubs for a while. If you filled in for her, you must have been close. Moana took pride in her work. She wouldn't trust her reputation with just anyone."

Harley nodded. "I figured we were friends."

"Don't you know?"

Harley twisted her hands in her lap. "I don't remember anything before last night. I had an accident. When I woke up, I was in this man's house dressed in a skimpy biker-chick costume."

Joy smirked. "Biker chick? That's not like Moana. This bachelor party must have been special order."

Grant shifted uncomfortably. Steve may have been the groom and man-of-honor at the get-together, but Harley's act had been shaped from Grant's most secret fantasies. Even the music she would have danced to hailed from his college days, when he used to wait for Gus to leave for class, then crank up the volume and sing the lyrics at the top of his lungs.

"You can't remember anything?"

Joy's question broke his revelry. Thankfully. Another few seconds and he'd be dragging Harley out to the truck without finding out a single fact about Moana—and not caring.

"The doctor said amnesia," Harley answered. "That's why I'm so anxious to find Moana. She's my only link to my life before last night."

Joy stood, crossed to the front of the desk, then folded her arms beneath her breasts. She pursed her bottom lip and looked Harley dead in the eye. Harley sat back and met her stare for stare, without an ounce of the apprehension Grant had seen in her just minutes ago in the truck. Her fears seemed to manifest only when they were alone.

He didn't have time to wonder why.

"Okay, I buy your story. Besides, neither one of you looks anything like the goons who've been asking around for Moana."

"Goons?" Harley's cheeks paled so discreetly, Grant assumed even Joy's appraising gaze would miss the subtle change.

"Probably pals of her boyfriend, Buck. He's a real scumbucket, you know? Anyway, they've been hitting all the local joints looking for Moana. They came here night before last. I was off, but Carl warned me. Moana's my friend. I don't want to cause her trouble."

"If she's your friend and I'm her friend, why don't you know me?"

Joy shrugged, slipped a nail file out of the pen holder on the desk and tended to her long, gold-tipped fingers. "No clue. Moana never mentioned anyone I didn't know."

"What about family?" Grant remained silent long enough. The pulsating rhythms of the music in the club, coupled with his renewed memories of his college musings made staying in this place painful, in a distinctly male fashion.

Leaning back on the desk, Joy shook her head. "She never talked much about family. Left home at sixteen. Something about her mother. She had a couple of cousins she missed a lot, but she only talked about that stuff when she drank. Which wasn't often."

"Do you know where she lives? Where we can find her?"

Joy hesitated, again scrutinizing Harley with a narrowed gaze. Fiercely protective, Joy was a friend Moana was lucky to have. Grant hoped she'd offer the same consideration to Harley.

Twisting around, Joy snatched a slip of paper and pen from the desk and scribbled. She handed the note to Harley. "Here's her phone number and address. She lives on Davis Island, just past downtown. She's supposedly out of town until next week, but you can leave her a message. If she knows you like I think she does, she'll call you back."

Harley reached out to shake Joy's hand. "I appreciate your trust. We won't abuse it, I promise."

Grant watched a smile bloom on Joy's sophisticated lips and wondered how on earth he'd ever thought he could steel himself against Harley's charm. In just one day, she'd enchanted both his secretary and this less-than-trusting exotic dancer. Of course, he'd been enraptured in just a matter of seconds the night before. And the spell hadn't lessened in the least. If anything, it had strengthened.

Grant took another piece of paper from the desk and wrote his unlisted phone number. "If you hear from Moana, or see her, tell her to call right away. I live in Citrus Hill. Harley's very anxious to hear from her."

Standing, he tugged on his pants to keep his renewed craving for Harley his little secret. Joy smirked, then tucked the folded paper in her palm. "I can handle that."

He still held the fifty-dollar bill in his hand, but didn't offer it for fear of insulting her. "Are you sure I can't offer you anything in exchange for your help?"

Joy's smile continued as she strode to the door. "Stay for the show and put that cash to good use. Couples come in this place all the time. The act before mine is a killer—the Diablo Sisters, Dina and Denise. They'll knock your socks off." Her appraising gaze traveled from Harley to Grant and back to Harley. Her grin turned sly. "Or other articles of clothing. Never know. You might just learn something."

With that, she exited. Grant cleared his throat and tried not to let his imagination run wild. Only a few feet away existed a window into his erotic dreams. His mouth dried at the thought of slipping into some darkened corner table with Harley and watching the Diablo Sisters weave their carnal magic. The education they might receive would be worth the price of a hefty tip.

Or better yet, he and Harley could spin some carnal magic of their own. Conduct private lessons.

"Do you want to stay?" Harley asked, startling Grant with the hint of curiosity clear in her voice.

"I'm male, Harley. The question is, do you want to stay?"

Part of her did. Perhaps she wanted to see firsthand what kind of dancer she'd been. More than likely, she wanted to see how the act affected Grant. His sexuality fascinated her. Ensnared her. Piqued her curiosity about her own needs and desires. Just watching his suppressed reactions to the lust so blatantly displayed around them renewed the spiraling tendrils of heat coursing through her.

But she wanted him to respond to her with more

than just lust—more than just instinctive male desire. Perhaps she'd had too much of that in her former life. Perhaps she hadn't deserved anything more from the men she danced for. Perhaps she hadn't wanted more. Now, she did. Suddenly, watching the dancers on stage lost all appeal.

"We should go by Moana's place." She held the folded address toward him, noticing the paper had wilted in her moistened grip.

"At this hour? Even a phone call should wait 'til morning."

Harley slipped the paper into her purse, thankful the action could cover her tiny grin. If Grant was so anxious to get rid of her, wouldn't he pound on Moana's door no matter the hour? At least insist they place the call before they left the club?

She could have been wrong about his motives. Maybe he really only wanted to help find out who she was—not because of his circumstances, but because of hers. She needed her past and her memories before she could regain her life.

But at this moment, she only needed Grant. "Then I'd like to go back to your place."

As he nodded and grabbed the doorknob, a hint of disappointment flitted across his features like a shadow. He wanted her as much as she wanted him. The evidence was as clear as the bulge in his slacks. But she couldn't see either one of them admitting to their desire aloud. He had his career to protect—and his conscience. So long as she remained unsure of herself, Grant Riordan would keep his distance.

And so long as she remained unsure of herself, she couldn't allow him to take any more risks than he already had. She had enough trouble justifying his sacrifices, excusing his risks.

She crossed in front of him and headed straight for the side door exit. Odds were that by morning, she'd be on her way home and out of his life forever—with or without her memory intact. If Moana turned out to be a friend like Harley suspected, she'd have no need to rely on Grant's hospitality further.

And yet, the thought of never knowing the depth of Grant's desire gnawed at her more than the possibility of never rediscovering who, or even if, anyone missed her.

HARLEY DECLINED GRANT'S invitation to join him in a late-night swim. She already felt herself on the verge of drowning. What she needed was a relentless workout. Her muscles screamed to be stretched out and pumped up. The monumental tension building in every fiber of her body had to be burned away. She must have been a regular fitness freak.

If only she had the nerve to initiate a workout that would satisfy her need for Grant.

Last night, she'd gone to Grant's room, not for seduction, but for comfort. The passion she'd experienced in his bed came in a wave of surprise and desperation. Tonight was different. She now knew the kind of man he was. Powerful yet kind. Driven yet selfless. Controlled yet secretly wild.

And it was his wild side she longed to see in a more natural habitat.

She'd dialed Moana's number from the kitchen phone as soon as they returned home. When an answering machine with a standard, mechanical voice answered, she hung up. Why disturb this woman in the middle of the night, if she was home at all? Harley wanted Moana to help her, not hate her. She resolved to try again in the morning, when her own attention was better focused.

After slipping into a knit tank top and shorts she'd purchased this afternoon, she grabbed a towel from the bathroom and headed to the home gym she'd found during her exploration of his house. Fully equipped with free weights, a padded floor, full-length wall mirrors and various Nautilus machines whose every purpose she knew, the workout room would provide a total exercise experience.

In the living room, she perused the CD storage unit, searching for something upbeat. She recognized the artists and titles—even some obscure ones—and for the briefest instant, she wondered why she couldn't remember something as simple as her real last name. She stopped and closed her eyes tightly, trying to burst through the brick wall erected between her and her memory.

It was no use. Though she'd cracked a chink or two, the barrier remained intact. Pushing herself did nothing but give her a headache.

But the pain in her temples disappeared when she caught sight of the perfect music for her workout. In the morning, she'd worry about her real name and her real life. Tonight would be about fantasy. About things you want, but know you can't have. About opening a window when Fate slams the door.

She grabbed the CD and headed to the back of the house.

GRANT DOVE BENEATH the water and swam the full length of the pool. When he reached the shallow end, he flipped and pushed off in the opposite direction, deciding not to surface until he had his emotions under control. By the time he reached the other end, he reconsidered. He couldn't hold his breath that long.

Instead he came up for air beneath the diving board. Grasping the fiberglass, he lifted himself up and down several times, wishing the cool water that dripped down and completely surrounded his body would ease the incessant ache constricting his groin.

No such luck. Nothing could ease his pain except Harley.

If she hadn't regained her memory, he couldn't touch her. He couldn't be responsible for taking advantage of a woman who might be married, engaged or the mother of four kids who still cried for her. No matter his personal discomfort, he had to keep his hands to himself—at least until he found out whether or not he had the right to claim her.

Once again he submerged, this time spanning the pool leisurely, trying to think only of the wetness surrounding him instead of how wet he would make her when the time came. He'd secretly hoped she'd reconsider his offer to join him in the pool. He'd even stuffed the condom Gus had left him in the small pocket of his swimming trunks before his conscience berated him for such a presumptuous action. Maybe it was better she'd said no. Floating beside her amid the sensual lapping waves, he never would have been able to control himself.

Reaching the pool's stairs, he swung himself around as he emerged, balancing on the edge and facing away from the house. He'd been in the water for nearly half an hour and the chlorine he'd recently added stung his eyes. When he twisted around and grabbed his towel, he noticed the lights in his home gym were on and the stereo pounded at full capacity, rattling the wall of glass doors.

He dried the water off his face and nearly choked.

Dressed in tiny gray shorts and a snug tank top tied below braless breasts, Harley relentlessly worked his Stairmaster. Her demanding pace, in double time against the steady, pounding beat of the music, spoke to the passion he'd already witnessed in her so many times. Her body glistened with a thin sheen of sweat. A triangle of perspiration soaked the back of her shorts. Her thighs and calves, bare and tan, constricted with each downward step, accentuating her sculpted muscles and smooth, tight skin.

Grant tossed the towel aside and submerged himself once again. His own muscles cramped as if he worked out alongside her. His lungs burned for air just as his hands burned to touch her, his lips to kiss her, his sex to bury deep inside her. Still, he forced himself to rise slowly, bracing his feet firmly on the pool's tiled floor.

He shook his hair, surprised at the new sensitivity of his flesh. Each and every droplet of water tickled as it glided down his back and chest. He only wished the sensation came from Harley's fingertips instead of from cold pool water.

He didn't need a genie to make that wish come true. *Just make the first move. She wants you as much as you want her.* Every signal, every sign revealed her mutual desire—her incredible hunger.

Yet he held back. Not just because of his job or his overwhelming sense of correctness.

He feared Harley. She embodied his most secret desires, his most delicious fantasies. With as little as a glance, she picked at him like a master locksmith. Once the door to his needs opened, how could he ever contain the passion he'd shut away?

And once he let her in, would he ever manage to release her?

Just at that moment, Harley looked over. With the lights glaring inside and the pool area darkened, he knew she couldn't see him. Still, she knew he was there.

Watching her.

Wanting her.

The reflection of that knowledge shaded her hooded gaze. She adjusted the tension gage on the control panel until her steps on the Stairmaster slowed, but didn't stop. Her actions became more deliberate, wrenching the maximum tension from her straining muscles. Her breathing slowed. Her breasts rose to a tantalizing peak as she inhaled long and deep. She tilted her head back and arched her spine, practically inviting him to ponder the roundness of her breasts, the generosity of her cleavage.

He braced himself at the edge of the pool and pulled himself out in one swift movement. Without a second thought to the towel or the water or his fears, he took long strides to the sliding glass door. Only then did he register the song blaring over his stereo system.

George Michael's "I Want Your Sex."

7

HE OPENED THE DOOR. Her timed steps on the exerciser faltered, but she recovered before he slipped over the threshold. A breath of warm night air pushed through the air-conditioning, embraced her, and left her panting. Yet the heat and the strain and the sweat didn't matter.

Grant wanted her. If he didn't, he wouldn't have come inside the gym. He could have easily slipped out of the pool and gone upstairs without disturbing her workout.

But he didn't. He wanted her—hopefully as much as she wanted him.

He stalked slowly, accelerating her heartbeat with his every step. She watched his progress in the mirrors across from her. Pool water darkened the carpet where he stepped. His hair, slicked back and dripping, curled around the corded muscles of his neck. His chest and abs bore the clear signs of a devotion to exercise—something she'd guessed at when snuggled against him the night before, but never could have verified until he'd shed his conservative career clothing. Nearly naked, eerily silent and obviously aroused, this approaching man showed little resemblance to the Grant she'd met at his office, or who'd accompanied her to the strip clubs. His eyes were darker. His nostrils flared. His mouth curved with hunger.

His wild side had emerged.

When he stood directly behind her like a shadow, the mingled scents of chlorine and natural musk overrode her senses. He shook his head, sprinkling her with cool droplets, showering her with lusty rain.

Music pounded in her ears. She slowed her stair climbing to a steady crawl.

"I'd forgotten this CD," he said, his voice low and rumbling, yet clear over the braying beat.

"It's perfect for a workout."

"You've been pushing yourself. Aren't you worn out?"

She stopped and stepped off the machine. Her shoulders touched his chest and chilled her with dripping pool water.

"I'm just getting started."

Without facing him, she slid away from the Stairmaster to a hulking Nautilus gleaming with polished chrome. She grasped the elongated handle above her head and pulled down, testing the stack of weights attached to the other end. She adjusted the tension level by resetting the pin, and then took the bar again. Wrapped in black foam rubber and suspended from a silver pulley, the bar was thick in her small hands—forcing her to assess the outline of Grant's wet swim trunks as he joined her.

"You could hurt yourself if you don't know what you're doing," he warned, again advancing at a lazy pace.

"I know what I'm doing."

She pulled the bar down halfway, sucking in air at the burning tautness in her arms.

"Care to share the knowledge?" He spoke from directly behind her, his breath coiling around her neck and shoulders, sending a tingle skittering across her skin. "I'm eager to learn."

With a muffled grunt, she eased the bar completely down and held it steady at her waist. Her arms shook, her heartbeat pounded. The strain reddened her face. "So am I."

She released the weight quickly, sending the stack of steel weights clanking down. Spinning to face him, she jumped, not just because of the metallic clatter of falling weights. His brown eyes, so comforting the night before, were nearly black with raw need.

"This could be a dangerous lesson to learn." The muscles in his neck, shoulders and arms tightened. His stone-written rules of responsibility and duty could easily destroy the tenuous cord of desire binding them together.

If she let them.

"Tell me what you want. *Honestly.*" She hid her shaking hands behind her back, twining her fingers into a tight knot. "Forget about my amnesia. Forget about your job. Forget about everything except how you feel right now. This moment."

His darkly lashed lids lowered until his eyes were nearly closed. His breath came in a ragged shudder. "At this moment, I want to make love to you."

Tentatively, she laid her flattened palms on his pecs, savoring his rapid heartbeat. "I want to make love with you. Now. Tonight. Who I am or who I'm not doesn't matter. I'm making a choice. I choose to be with you."

With amazing gentleness, he wrapped his large hands around her trembling fingers. "Harley, we don't know the fire we're playing with. We could both get very burned."

She adored his talent for being the voice of reason, even when reason didn't apply. "Burn me, Grant. I want the heat. Don't you?"

With a growl that stopped her heart, Grant grabbed

Harley's buttocks, her hands still twined with his, and thrust her against him. His lips and tongue attacked hers like a starved beast—stealing the air from her lungs. Full and hard, his erection jammed against her belly. He lifted her and pressed her even closer, forcing her body's throbbing rhythm to match his own.

Liquid heat frothed inside her. Her nipples bit through her sopping tank top, aching for the moisture only he could give. When he tore his mouth away from hers and greedily kissed and bit and soothed her neck and shoulders, she gasped. Her eyes flew open. The room spun in a Technicolor whirl.

Trapping her arms behind her, he maneuvered both her hands into one of his, freeing his other to slip beneath her shorts and knead her backside. When he found the flimsy strip of lace panties, he twisted his fingers around the side strap and tugged until they ripped apart. Though he sucked the exposed skin just above her nipples with furious urgency, he removed the torn underwear slowly, pulling from behind so the sandpaper texture of the lace scraped through her sensitive flesh like a thousand tiny fingertips.

"Oh, Grant."

He tugged her panties free from her shorts and tossed them aside, then kissed his way back to her mouth. With gentle teeth, he nipped at her lips, licked her, withholding his mouth from hers until she fought his grip.

His chuckle resonated through her. "You wanted to burn. Let me show you my version of fire." He raised her arms above her head and hooked them over the suspended bar. "Are you game?"

In his eyes, she witnessed a promise of true pleasure, a vow to cast away every bond, every wall that might keep them from achieving complete intimacy. He sought to open himself to her—and to do so by bringing her over the edge of her own desires. By the end of the night, she would know him better than anyone. Perhaps, she'd even know herself.

"I told you last night, Grant. I trust you."

His smile touched every inch of his rugged face—except his eyes. They remained serious. Focused. Intense. "Then, hang on, honey." He wrapped her fingers around the foam rubber bar, then kissed her knuckles. "Don't let go. No matter what. Think you can do that?"

She could only nod and tighten her grip. Wicked intentions now danced in his eyes, and the anticipation of his loving made her skin prickle with gooseflesh.

His hot tongue burned a trail down the stretched muscles of her left arm, then dipped into the side of her tank top, laving the outer swell of her breast. His hands spanned her bare midriff, his palms scorching her belly, his fingertips teasing her rib cage under her shirt. Kissing across the thin material of her shirt, he surrounded one nipple with his mouth and sucked until the nub puckered and strained. Warm moisture seeped through the cotton, promising an even deeper pleasure once she was topless.

She squirmed, her body throbbing. He made no move to undress her and she considered letting go of the bar and removing her shirt. Yet his look of clear warning made her grip the bar even tighter.

"You have the most perfect body." He formed his words against her skin, complimenting and arousing her at the same time. He pressed her breasts together and alternately attended one nipple, then the other. "I want to see you. Up close."

"Mmm. Please."

He slipped his hands out of her shirt and snapped

the thin shoulder straps. "How much did you pay for this shirt again?"

She shook her head. She couldn't remember. She didn't care. She just wanted his wet mouth on her aching nipples. She wanted him to taste her, knead her, drive her to complete mindlessness. "A dollar. Two maybe."

"I can afford another." He kissed her neck. "Hold on."

He tore at the stretchy cotton. When the material didn't immediately give way, he dug in with his fingers and pulled until she heard a welcomed rip. Again, he slid the material away slowly, like the shedding of skin. Under the weight of his hungry gaze, her breasts seemed fuller, rounder.

He stepped back. "Absolutely perfect." He perused her nakedness leisurely, appreciatively, making her feel more beautiful than she'd thought possible. Moisture pooled between her legs and her thighs quivered. "But I want to see all of you. All at once."

If he looked to her for approval, she missed it. Her eyes drifted closed in heightened expectation. Her knuckles ached as she clung to the bar. A long moment passed before she felt his hands on her again, grasping the waistband of her shorts.

He tugged slowly, kissing her bared hip, her inset navel, the top of one thigh, the inside of her knee. The material dropped to the floor. He lifted one ankle and then the other, seducing her instep while he slipped her shorts away.

Instinctively, she drew her legs together, fighting the building pressure at the apex of her thighs. He chuckled and slid her ankles apart just enough to allow the cool breeze from the vent above to mingle with her warm feminine moisture.

"I said I wanted to see all of you, sweetheart." He knelt before her, his murmur sending a hot burst of air skittering through her curls. "Exquisite."

Without warning, he took her in his mouth, bracing his hands on her buttocks and pressing her to him fully. She gasped and held her breath while bolts of lightning crisscrossed her inner eyelids and then traveled down each and every nerve. Weakened, she fought to hold the bar. If she let go, she'd break the magic spell he wove with his mouth.

His tongue swirled within her while his hands smoothed up her legs. She whimpered, her eyelids flying open when he pinched her buttocks, lightly, but enough to bring her full attention to the needs of her lower body. The contrast between the pain of his tweaks and the sweet gentleness of his tongue made her cry out his name.

He hummed his approval inside her, then lifted her right knee and slung it over his shoulder, tilting her to a perfect angle for his loving. "Scream out, honey. Tell me what you like. Tell me if you want more."

She could hardly think while his tongue plundered and his fingers plucked. She'd never imagined such delight.

"More. Yes, more."

He pinched her harder and slipped his tongue deeper, discovering the pinpoint of her need. Her cry reverberated over the music of the forgotten CD. She gasped for air when he slipped one hand between her legs to aid his mouth in pleasuring her. One finger and then two slid inside until she could no longer contain the pressure.

In moments, she was lost. Her arms went limp, but her hands held fast. She shook and shuddered and cried with the explosion. His mouth never abandoned her—not even after the convulsions ceased. Then, gently, he kissed his way up to her mouth, pried her hands free from the bar and lifted her into his arms.

She forced her eyes open, her eyelids fluttering against the suddenly harsh light. "Where are we going?"

He placed a tiny kiss on the tip of her nose. "Not far."

A few feet away, he released her, sliding her down the rigid length of his body. Still wobbly, her legs barely supported her weight. He sat on the edge of the low cushioned bench beside his free weights and leaned back against the tilted padding.

He held his hand out to her, but she hesitated, enjoying the view of his long, lean torso. Toned and glistening with a mixture of perspiration and pool water, his body was large and hard and perfect. Though spent, she ached to see him naked, to feel him deep inside.

He folded his hands behind his head, his grin cocksure. "Second thoughts?"

She shook her head, licking her lips like he had just minutes—or was it hours?—before. Spotting the switch on the mirror, she lowered the lights to a warm amber glow.

"You're overdressed."

He laughed, and the sound compelled her more than the rhythmic beat still blaring from the stereo. Unbound, Grant laughed and smiled and took and gave with such abandon, her heart swelled. And her body craved him even more.

Now would be her turn to give.

He discarded his shorts quickly, pulled something from the pocket, then reclined on the workout bench and laced his hands behind his head once more. He waited for her to make the next move, as if he relished relinquishing control.

She bit her bottom lip, suddenly shy and unsure. She hadn't planned this seduction, but she'd done everything she could to encourage him. He hadn't disappointed her. She felt alive. Powerful. Her incredible climax still reverberated through her tingling skin. How could she ever reciprocate with equal skill?

"Harley, come here."

She obeyed, nearly floating on the intimate wave of his voice. He pulled up on his elbows, and his eyes narrowed just enough for her to sense his scrutiny. Without a word, he held out his hand, captured her, and reeled her in.

Of her own volition, she kneeled beside him and closed her eyes, drowning in the warm tide of his closeness. He lazily ran a finger up the outside of her arm, then across her collarbone and down to her breast.

"I love touching you."

She took his hint. Starting at his ankle, she smoothed her palm up his calf and over his knee, burying her fingers in the dark hair shadowing his powerful thighs. She glanced up when he reclined, his face a mask of rapture, but then concentrated again on exploring him with complete fascination.

He groaned when she surrounded his sacs with a gentle caress. When she traced his shaft from hilt to tip, he gasped aloud and breathed her name. Emboldened, she wrapped her entire hand around him.

He'd stopped touching her, and yet she yearned for him. Her mouth watered, her breasts ached, her body quivered at the realization she'd soon have him inside her. Deep inside. Touching her where she felt sure she'd never been touched—connecting with her on a plane far beyond her comprehension.

But first, she'd know every inch of him, just as he now knew her. Without a second thought, she took him in her mouth. His moans became a music more sensual and suggestive than any she'd ever heard. She spanned his chest with her hands, plucked at his peaked nipples, measured his pounding heart beneath her moistened palms.

"Harley, I need you. Now."

He positioned her to straddle him, balancing her on his thighs. Tearing open the condom he'd snatched from his shorts, Grant sheathed himself quickly then grasped her hips and slid her forward until his tip teased her.

"Tell me you want this, sweetheart. Tell me now or…"

She placed two fingers over his mouth, braced her other hand on his shoulder and closed her eyes. She wanted Grant so fiercely, with such concentrated longing, she knew she'd never experienced such desire. A need so intimate and yet so extreme could never be forgotten. Never.

Grant was her chivalrous rescuer, saving her from the evil nothingness—a fantasy lover with whom reality could never exist, but a dream could be nirvana. She had one chance, one night to scorch the essence of his power into her hungry soul.

She scooted back, guiding him inside her. "Make me never forget."

"Either that, or I'll die trying."

Grabbing her by the hips, he entered swiftly. She cried out again, startled by his thick length—and by her own tightness. Her body encircled his with the snugness of a woman whose last lover was in the distant past.

But she couldn't spare the brainpower to decipher the contradiction between her profession and her inexperience. She could think of nothing else but going with Grant to the height of ecstasy.

"Oh, Grant."

He forced his eyes open. Wonder flushed her skin from her cheeks to her breasts, darkening her nipples and widening her eyes. Grant knew being inside her would be beyond his wildest dreams—but reality left him breathless. He cupped her supple buttocks and pressed her down, hissing choked air through clenched teeth as she descended his length.

She was tight. Not virgin tight, but her inner muscles clamped around him, milking him with the sweet spasms of a woman who hadn't been made love to nearly enough, but who relished the sensations now. His heart swelled as fully as his shaft. Harley didn't fear the self-surrender real lovemaking demanded. She embraced the experience. Challenged it. Pushed their desires past all limits and expectations.

He'd never known such ecstasy.

He drove deeper until he could go no further, then braced his feet on the ground, pulled in his knees and sat up completely. She screamed again and tossed her head back, groaning as he ground his sex into hers. Cupping her buttocks, he suckled her breasts as the new angle increased their pleasure. Raging heat surged inside him. They'd reached the precipice. He wouldn't last much longer.

Using her thighs to match his movements, Harley plunged with her own power, stroking him with her body, loving him straight to his soul. She discovered a stirring rhythm, then played, faster and faster until Grant felt the room rock.

"Harley, I, oh," he muttered before seizing her mouth with his and lifting his body off the bench, fusing them to the core.

"Yes, Grant, yes." Her shouts urged him, begged him to come with her into the insanity of fruition.

Easing her backward, he cradled her spine, laid her on the weight bench and drove one final time. Liquid heat poured out of him, accompanied by a liberating bellow that burned his lungs and throat. His eyes sprang open, but he could see nothing but a dizzying halo of prismed light.

In the center of the rainbow, Harley smiled.

He remained inside her, panting, unable and unwilling to speak. She curled her arms around his neck, tangling her fingers in his damp hair, splaying light kisses along his collarbone and neck. Slowly, the tension eased and Grant's legs and back cramped. Still, he didn't move. For the briefest of moments, he considered staying inside her forever.

"Ow."

Her tiny protest, spoken as she attempted to shift her position on the bench, spurred him to see to her comfort. He disentangled her legs from around his hips and scooted back, straddling the bench. "Sorry, honey."

She frowned when he pulled away, a sweet little pucker of lips that reminded him of a spoiled child. He couldn't help grinning.

"What are you smirking at?" she asked.

He braced his hands on her waist and helped her sit up. "At you. At that face."

Coiling her arms around his neck, she shifted her legs back around his waist and pulled herself forward.

Her nipples, still peaked and hard, rubbed his chest. A fragrant steam seemed to waft from her skin. Still warm and wet from their lovemaking, she pressed against him boldly. Amazingly, he stiffened in response.

"I only had one condom, Harley."

She sighed and kissed him on the jawbone. "What a shame."

Snuggling her soft cheek against his chest, Grant closed his eyes and cursed his conservative life-style. Guys like his brother, Gus, or best friend, Mac, probably kept dozens of prophylactics on hand for just this kind of emergency. But not Grant. Oh, no. He'd thrown out his supply along with his wedding photos. Like the pictures, they only reminded him of his meager sex life.

He kissed the top of her head. "A crying shame, sweetheart. And unfortunately, Wellesley Manor residents voted down the proposed all-night convenience store. Attracts too much riffraff."

Her deep-throated chuckle warmed him, contrasting with the gooseflesh prickling her skin. He rubbed her back vigorously, inhaling a sensual scent he'd forever associate with the best night of his life—and with the amazing woman who radiated the sweet, musky fragrance. Despite the spent condom still covering him, the chilly atmosphere of the air-conditioning, and the solid knowledge that they couldn't make love again tonight—at least not with some semblance of safety—a rush of renewed passion surged through him.

He'd started calculating time and distance to the nearest twenty-four hour drugstore outside his neighborhood when Harley traced the shell of his ear with a tongue-moistened finger and then whispered to him, "Other things don't necessarily need a condom."

Two seconds, maybe three, passed before he thought of several delicious possibilities. "I like the way you think."

"Then what are we waiting for? Let's not waste another minute."

8

THE *KAMA SUTRA* came in handy. Resigned to save the chapters on sexual positions for another time, Grant ended his night of fantasy with Harley by practicing several different forms of sensual touching. By candlelight, she'd recited arousing passages in her deep sultry voice while he massaged every inch of her with a sweet-smelling oil he'd found in his downstairs guest bathroom. He discovered her ticklish spot behind her knee and a star-shaped birthmark on her pert rear end.

He also learned how much he adored her breasts. Round and creamy white. Dark areolas. Rock hard nipples. And sensitive. With only the palm-warmed oil and his hungry hands and mouth, he'd caressed and pinched and laved her to a slow but searing climax.

Then she'd returned the favor. She'd found erogenous spots on his body he never knew existed. Her hands made him delirious; her mouth drove him over the edge. If not for the unfairness to Harley, he would have ignored his principles regarding safe sex and made love to her without the half-dozen condoms he would have needed to satisfy his appetite.

Instead, their private lessons taught them all the exotic ways of loving. By sunrise when he'd tucked her in his bed and stroked her until she fell asleep, Grant knew and worshipped every inch of Harley's body— every pulse point—every erotic zone. The knowledge would stay with him forever, no matter what he discovered about her identity when he took her to Moana's apartment after the wedding.

Too keyed up to nap more than an hour, Grant sneaked out of bed early, showering and dressing without rousing Harley from her fitful sleep. Once, she'd struggled with a disturbing dream, but by the time he reached her side, she'd settled down. His heart had stopped in that quiet moment. Had she remembered something distressing, something ugly from her past? Was Gus right that her conscious mind kept dark memories silent behind a blank wall? Whatever the situation, Grant swore he wouldn't allow Harley to return to any life not worthy of her special magic. After the rapture she'd brought to him, he'd move the sun and the moon to ensure her happiness.

Unwilling to wake her so early, he scribbled another quick note and left it on her pillow, grabbed his keys and headed to Tampa to pick up his tuxedo for the wedding.

Of course, he stopped at the drugstore first.

The drive to Tampa was short, just under half an hour. Westbound traffic on I-4 moved quickly, while the eastbound side chugged along with tourists heading toward Orlando's numerous attractions. Grant set the cruise control at 65 miles per hour and watched the road while orange groves and strawberry fields rolled by on either side.

Having made this drive more times than he could count, his mind replayed the last forty-eight hours—and anticipated the next. Though he'd found Moana's phone number on the kitchen table before he left, he resisted the urge to call. As much as he wanted Harley to regain her memory and start piecing together her past, he couldn't bear the thought of her leaving. Surely, he could use his Phi Beta Kappa intellect to figure out how to keep Harley in his life and prevent him from losing his job if someone discovered her past.

But the solution couldn't involve lies. Lies always unraveled. Always. His review of his time with Harley was a prime example. He'd convinced himself and the world that he was a serious, dedicated professional who'd do nothing to jeopardize his career, no matter the cost to his personal life or happiness. Yet in less than two days, he'd exposed his truest longings and acted out his favorite fantasies with a woman he hadn't known long enough to trust, but did.

He'd never done anything so wonderfully irresponsible. And he had no one in particular to blame for the sameness of his life but himself. His parents never *made* him the responsible child to offset Gus's foibles. They were loving, freethinking intellectuals who found silver linings in the darkest clouds. Grant chose to be the reliable, steady son, basking in the shine of his parent's pride and his importance in the family.

In school, Grant had done the same—picking the role of model student instead of falling in with the slightly less savory and definitely more interesting guys who drove fast cars and celebrated D's with the same thrill as he did A's. He'd played tennis and golf instead of football. Studied economics rather than shop. Dated debutantes instead of cheerleaders.

Even his marriage had been more of a logical next step than a reflection of love or lasting passion. Camille had been beautiful, of course, but in a cool, refined way. Their pairing was mutually beneficial rather than exciting or passionate or impulsive. Despite his secret fantasies, even his lovemaking with Camille never strayed from the predictable. When it had once, in his attempt to avoid an inevitable divorce, Camille had called him a pervert.

Considering the source, the insult was more a reflection of her hang-ups than his, and solidified his decision to end his counterfeit marriage before he lost his sanity. But instead of using the split as impetus to a sorely needed life change, he fell back into the same old reputable rut.

Until last night. Until Harley.

She possessed no more knowledge than any other woman he'd known, but her open abandon and sexual curiosity spurred him to shed all inhibitions and ignore every possible consequence. Nothing had mattered but pleasing her. Learning her. Learning about himself.

In the morning's light, he recognized the risk he'd taken. Though Harley would never intentionally hurt him or his career, her presence alone could set enough tongues wagging to bring his prosperity to a complete stop. Disclosing her presence to his neighbor, even innocently, could have already started his downward momentum. Yet she had done her best to allay Mrs. Langley's suspicions with logical explanations that sounded nothing like the lies they were. He admired her inventiveness. Hell, after last night, he practically worshipped it. He could get used to having Harley around on a long-term, daily basis.

The thought startled him. He tapped his brake unnecessarily, causing the driver behind him to sound his horn and pull around him, flashing the universal sign of displeasure.

How could he ask Harley to stay in his world—one that would eventually drain her of the very qualities he coveted?

The answer was—he couldn't.

Grant shook himself, pressed the gas pedal and resumed his normal speed. If only he could resume his normal life as easily. Never mind that he didn't want his old life or his old ways back. Never mind how the lies exhausted him, ate at him with more fury than any ulcer.

Even if he wanted to abandon his controlled and conservative life, he couldn't. Not yet. Nanna Lil needed him. So did Gus. What little he had in the way of family roots were grown in Citrus Hill. He couldn't deny that just because of his hormones. Of course, he wouldn't be trapped here forever. Circumstances would change. But by then, Harley would be long gone.

He clicked on the CD player. On a whim, he'd grabbed the George Michael disc from the gym before he'd left. The sound of reverent organ music, the prelude to the title track, filled the car. As the British rocker started to sing about "faith," a plan formed. Maybe he and Harley couldn't have a future, but the here and now—at least for today—was wide open. With a little finesse, he could plant himself more firmly in Harley's present, and let the past and the future fend for themselves.

A DREAM. A MEMORY. This time, however, she didn't wake up. Too tired to struggle, too comfortable to fight, Harley let her mind drift deeper into the subconscious flash of pictures. A tiny bungalow, painted bright pink and sporting a seashell driveway, emerged in her mind's eye. Home. But not home. A place where she'd lived.

Suddenly inside the house, an uneasy tension crept through her. A fine antique lamp sat incongruously beside a plastic-covered couch. A magnificent Oriental carpet covered an unfinished terrazzo floor. Signs of tasteful opulence dotted a structure dominated by garage sale grabbers and questionable collectibles. Harley cringed at the final result.

Then she saw a face. A boy. Sixteen or so, with a shiny metal smile reflecting a computer screen's bright blue backdrop. Too young to be a lover, too old to be a son, this young man meant the world to her.

And she to him.

He missed her.

Harley struggled to stay within the dream, fought for a clearer picture of the boy whose name she couldn't summon. Instead, she found herself opening a closet. Her closet. Filled with costumes bedecked with spangles and feathers and translucent silks. She reached out, but the textures eluded her. She recognized the dresses as hers—but not hers. They belonged to someone else, or maybe, someone she used to be.

Tossing in Grant's bed, Harley felt the softness of his sheets against her bare skin. Yet the dream remained. Caught between two worlds, she struggled to see more—learn more—even if the knowledge meant losing Grant.

The thought brought her bolt upright. Sunlight stung her dry eyes. She rubbed the sleep away, but held fast to the images fresh in her mind. Once she settled back into the cushioned pillows and fluffy down comforter, she tried to piece the pictures together and form a memory or two.

She couldn't.

She gave up trying once she glanced at the alarm clock, which read eleven-fifteen. Though she and Grant hadn't gone to sleep until somewhere around dawn, she didn't expect to have slept so late. She'd wanted to call Moana's number early, before she had a chance to leave for the day—if she was in town at all.

She also had to figure out what to wear to the wedding this afternoon.

If Grant still wanted her to go. Despite last night, she wouldn't blame him for being uneasy about her appearing with him in public, forcing them to lie to so many people important to Grant's life and career. They'd shared a private freedom she'd always treasure, but that didn't mean they should announce their relationship to the uptight residents of Citrus Hill. Especially if she was who she suspected she was. A woman who stripped.

The venomous words of Wilhelmina Langley's column reverberated in her brain. Would the woman be any kinder to an exotic dancer than she had been to the paid-off prostitute? Harley dashed into the bathroom before she started composing provocative headlines in her head.

WHEN SHE EMERGED from the shower a half hour later, she found a private invitation to the wedding draped across the bed. She lifted the royal blue silk shift tentatively, allowing the soft lightness of the fabric to slide over her fingers. With matching shoes, bag and short jacket, the outfit would highlight both her eyes and her petite figure.

In a tissue-filled box beside the dress, Grant left her a cache of underthings that nearly made her blush. The clingy dress would barely hide the satiny thong panties, sleek demi-bra, smooth garter belt and stockings.

Just thinking of how sensual she'd feel in such decadent clothing, she let out a low, breathy whistle.

"My sentiments exactly."

Her body tingled from the raspy sound of Grant's voice. She turned to find him standing in the threshold, leaning his broad bare shoulder against the doorjamb and grinning wolfishly, as if she wore the lingerie instead of just a towel.

"You've been a busy shopper this morning."

She dropped the garter belt back into the box and held her towel tighter. His gaze raked over her with brazen need. Wearing only his tuxedo pants, unbuckled and swung low on his hips, his desire was more than evident. She wet her lips in anticipation. Had he stopped and bought condoms as he'd promised last night? Did they have time for a quick interlude? A glance at the clock told her noon had just passed. Her stomach rumbled, but an entirely different hunger filled her from head to toe.

"There was a full service dress shop adjacent to the tuxedo place. I hope you like my taste."

She smiled shyly, her blood cooling to a steady simmer. "The dress is perfect. You didn't have to go to such expense. I could have found something suitable in that box."

She glanced at the corner, surprised to see the carton of his ex-wife's hand-me-downs had disappeared.

"You deserve better than Camille's throwaways."

She threw you away, Harley thought ruefully. The woman had to be an utter fool.

He shoved his hands into his pockets. "I took the box to a donation drop-off on my way out."

Harley nodded, then ran her hand through her damp hair. She hadn't applied any makeup except her base and blush, and could only imagine how horrendous she must look. Judging from the expression in Grant's warm brown eyes, however, she couldn't look that bad. "Still want me to go to the wedding with you?"

To the wedding. To bed. To the ends of the Earth. Grant wondered if admitting that would wipe away the uncertainty that marred her vibrant blue eyes. How could a woman so alluring be so unsure of her charisma? He'd already given up trying to fight her charm. One flash of those baby blues and he was gone, gone, gone.

"I'd be honored to escort you to the wedding."

"What about our story about my being your cousin? Won't your friends spill the beans?"

"Not if they value their lives. They're all coming here to meet the limo. I'll make the rules perfectly clear then. Don't worry about me, Harley. I can take whatever comes."

"We shouldn't invite trouble."

"Too late."

She carefully refolded the lingerie, replaced the box lid and hugged the package to her chest. "I guess I'd better dress. You don't want the guys to get the wrong idea."

Grant pushed away from the jamb and kicked the door closed with his heel. "I wouldn't worry about their wrong ideas. Just mine."

Her smile glittered like a shooting star, burning away the doubtfulness he despised. When they made love, when he openly displayed his physical need for her, she blossomed like a flame in dry air. He wanted her to experience that power all the time, but knew she wouldn't until she rediscovered her past.

"I need to dry my hair." Her words stopped him at arm's length. He wouldn't force the issue. Maybe after last night, she needed a break.

She stepped into the master bathroom and tossed a coy glance over her shoulder.

"Want to watch?"

She didn't need to ask twice. In front of the wall-wide mirror, Grant pulled out the cushioned stool shoved beneath the vanity. He draped a towel over his forearm and invited her to sit.

"You don't have to help."

He began massaging her scalp with the soft terrycloth. "I'm not helping because I have to."

"I don't just mean now."

Glancing into the mirror, he wrapped the towel in his hands and rubbed it through her dark hair. "I'm not helping because I have to," he repeated, finding her gaze and locking it with his as he spoke.

She smiled, picked up a palette of eyeshadow and applied a skin-tone color while he rubbed the dampness from her hair. He pulled out the blow-dryer while she contoured her eyes with a darker shade of shadow and then applied mascara and lipstick. He watched her, fascinated. She did so little, but the result was startling. Her eyes appeared larger, her lips fuller. Her cheeks blossomed with the same hue as when they made love.

He plugged the dryer into the socket and zipped up his pants. His friends would arrive any minute. He couldn't surrender to the driving need stiffening his sex and fuddling his brain.

"I don't really know what to do with this."

She pulled a brush out of the drawer. "Just turn it on. I'll show you."

He chose a medium setting. She leaned her head back and closed her eyes, allowing the warm stream of air to flow freely through her hair. He couldn't resist combing his fingers through the strands.

When she picked up the brush, he followed her lead, focusing the air on the bristles, watching the haphazard array straighten into the style she favored. Her bangs softly framed her face, the sides kissed her cheeks alluringly, the back fanned her shoulders. As she laid the brush on the countertop, he clicked the dryer off.

"You make it look so easy."

"Years of practice." She spritzed her hair with a sweet-smelling spray and scooted back the stool.

"Hand me the box, won't you?"

He removed the top of the box and dug into the tissue. He knew she meant for him to leave while she dressed, but he didn't. Instead, he removed the thong panties and held them between two fingers. "I'd like to keep helping."

She stood, her hand locked on the knot of her towel. "Oh, you would, would you?"

"Well, these underthings cost nearly as much as my tuxedo. I'd like to see the entire ensemble. Piece by piece."

"In my line of work, don't men use their money to watch me *undress?*"

"I'm different."

She undid the knot and let the towel pool at her feet. "I can't argue with that."

He leaned against the vanity as she plucked the panties from his grip. Sitting again, she slipped her feet into the strips of satin and shimmied them up her shapely calves, over her knees, across her thighs. She stood, turned her back to him and completed the job, placing the thong securely between her cheeks.

"Which piece next?"

He snatched the bra from the box, tossed it over his shoulder and stepped behind her, turning her to the mirror. Cupping her breasts with his hands, he watched her nipples harden, watched her eyelids close and her lips slightly part. She felt so full and warm in his hands, he envied the lingerie.

"Is this what a bra feels like?" he asked, pressing her breasts upward, increasing her cleavage.

"Hardly," she rasped, cooing when he plucked her nipples playfully.

"Good." He slid the bra from his shoulder and guided her arms into the devilish contraption. "Then when you wear this—" he pulled the straps over her shoulders and hooked the clasps "—I want you to think about how much better my hands would feel."

He slipped his forefingers into the cups and adjusted them to cover her completely. Grazing her nipples again, he smiled when she moaned in delight.

"Can you imagine my hands all over you all night long?"

Her eyes fluttered open. "With the right incentive."

He traced the satin panties with a tentative touch, then placed his palm over her mons, applying just enough pressure to gauge how she heated beneath his hand.

Reaching back, she slid her hands around his neck, arched her back and pressed her buttocks against his erection. Despite his intention only to tease her, he dipped a finger into the tiny triangle of material, sliding through her curls to find her simmering center.

"Is this the incentive you mean?"

Grinding her backside against his sex, she lifted one leg atop the chair, easing his access.

"You're on the right track."

The doorbell sounded downstairs, breaking his rhythm and shattering the mood.

"Damn." He straightened Harley's panties as he nuzzled her neck. "They would be on time."

She twisted around in his arms and kissed him gently on the jaw. "Seems their timing is just right. The object was to get dressed, not undressed, remember?"

"I have a problem with that concept when you're around."

Slipping away, she pulled the stockings and garter belt out of the box and returned to the bedroom. "You have a lot of problems with me around."

The comment came matter-of-factly, but the words still punched him like a left hook to the gut. He'd been trying like hell to make Harley comfortable in his life, moving her things to his room, buying her a spectacular dress to wear to the wedding, not reminding her to call Moana again. From the bathroom, he watched her sit on his bed among a tangle of rumpled sheets and stretch the hose over her shapely legs. She snapped the garters in place with little fanfare and then stepped into the dress and strappy heels.

As incongruous and illogical as it sounded, she fit in his world more easily than he did. She adapted. She melded. Though he knew she felt the outsider as much as he, she hid her insecurities better—mainly because she didn't seem to mind closeting her true nature. At least not for the short term.

Yet he knew firsthand the agony of penning away one's real self. She'd shown him—first in the gym and then again in the bathroom. He'd seen how he'd been suppressing his needs—not really for sex as much as for intimacy. He'd tasted delights of utter abandon. With Harley he bared his soul—good and bad—and she neither labeled nor judged. Not like Camille. Not like his friends. Despite their respect for him, they expected Grant to behave one way and one way only. For him to test the waters beyond perfect respectability would throw them into complete shock.

The doorbell rang again. In a few minutes, he'd tell them he was taking the stripper to the wedding—Citrus Hill's high society event of the week. He could only imagine the reactions.

Dressed except for the coordinating jacket, Harley snapped him from his thoughts when she asked, "You want me to get that?"

"No. No. Take your time." He opened the bedroom door reluctantly, wanting more than anything to return to the timeless moment in the bathroom when nothing stood between them except the flimsy silk of her panties and bra. "I picked up lunch. It's in the kitchen. But don't take too long. The guys are known to wolf down large quantities of munchies in record time."

When he left, Harley plopped down on the bed, closed her eyes and exhaled. Her body still thrummed from his short-lived seduction in the bathroom—her heart's pounding drowned out the muted voices downstairs. Her presence undoubtedly caused Grant innumerable problems, but he wasn't so innocent either.

Whenever he so much as looked at her with the slightest longing, she transformed into a sex-starved hussy. Caught in a confused tangle between desire and the truth, Harley knotted herself deeper with every moment she spent with him.

She was falling in love with Grant Riordan.

Correction—she'd already hit bottom.

She hadn't meant to. Hadn't planned to. The idea had never crossed her mind. How could she fall in love with someone she'd known for only two days? And yet, how could she not? Despite the long list of reasons why he shouldn't have gotten involved with her, he had—from letting her stay in his home to making love to her. Now he even insisted on parading her in front of his major investors and his boss. What if she screwed up? What if one of those holier-than-thou socialites had once seen her act and recognized her? Without saying a word, she could ruin Grant forever.

Grant didn't know about her dream—her glimpse into her former life. The unrefined house and closet full of skimpy costumes gave her strong evidence that she'd never truly blend into Grant's world. While she might survive the wedding without harming his reputation, sooner or later, someone would discover her past and use her to hurt Grant.

Grant knew the risks and surprisingly, chose to take them. Maybe because he resented interference in his private life—maybe because he was tired of pretending to be someone he wasn't. But he couldn't just pick up and leave Citrus Hill. His family and responsibilities tied him here. Willingly. She'd seen the exorbitant bills from the renovation of his grandmother's house in his study and heard his Nanna's messages as they came over his answering machine.

Yet despite the overwhelming obligations, Grant spoke of his family, particularly Nanna Lil and Gus, with indisputable affection. She couldn't do anything to cause him to have to leave them. She just couldn't.

Sitting up, she slipped on her jacket, filled the tiny handbag with her compact and lipstick and headed down the back staircase to the kitchen. Pausing on the lowest step, she heard Grant's muffled voice in the living room, undoubtedly reading his friends the riot act. She couldn't decipher the words, but his tone made his seriousness clear. Her cheeks reddened.

She went into the kitchen unnoticed, snatched Moana's number from the counter and headed back upstairs. She dialed the number and again heard the answering machine that greeted her the night before. This time, she left a message.

"Moana, this is Harley. If you can, please be home this evening. I'm coming over. Around nine o'clock. I really, really need to see you."

The desperation in her voice surprised her. But her wonderful night with Grant proved one undeniable fact. If she wanted a future with him, however unlikely that might be, she had to stop running from her past. Remembering wasn't a distant possibility anymore. Her dream this morning proved her amnesia was slowly losing its grip. Confusing but clear, the images confirmed that her brain still kept her memories stored in some hard-to-reach place.

More than likely, she only needed one more gentle shove—one Moana might provide—to restore her murky past. Then, and only then, could she make decisions about her future.

9

AT THE RECEPTION HALL, the ceiling, archways and a forest of floral topiaries blinked and sparkled with a thousand tiny lights. Silver candelabras flickered from the center of each linen-covered table. Soft strains of a classical harp floated over the rose-scented air and champagne flowed as freely as an afternoon rain-shower. The antebellum clubhouse of the Citrus Hill Golf and Country Club radiated warmth and romance, despite the sea of eyes that assessed Harley from head to toe the minute she and Grant appeared in the entranceway.

Grant, who slipped her hand onto his arm before they entered, laid his palm over her knuckles. "Pay attention to the introductions. There will be a quiz at the end of the night."

His mock seriousness wrought a tentative smile from her tightly drawn lips. "I hope it's multiple choice. I always do better with multiple choice."

Grant chuckled, then suddenly stiffened. Harley followed the line of his gaze to a straight-postured, silver-haired man handing a glass of champagne to an equally stunning woman dressed in pale green sequins and wearing a diamond cocktail ring so large, Harley saw the sparkle from across the room.

"Mr. Phipps?" she guessed.

Grant nodded. "Howell and his wife, Amelia. They're talking with Bailey Ford, the founding partner of Ford, Rienholt and Long. Attorneys. Very well connected. Very conservative. One of our largest investors."

From a distance, the men appeared more impressive than intimidating. Both men undoubtedly wielded great power over many people, yet when Harley compared them to the man beside her, she had no doubt Grant would someday make the older men's combined success pale in comparison. She only had to ensure that she—and the power players at the other end of the dining hall—didn't keep him from getting his shot.

Smiling at a waiter, Harley was immediately offered a tray of champagne flutes. She tugged Grant's sleeve to snatch his attention away from his boss. "Here's our fortification." She handed him a glass, then took one for herself, clinking her rim to his. "I suggest the direct approach."

"You would."

"Hasn't failed me yet. So far, I've enjoyed innumerable results from simply going after what I want." Her mind drifted back to his seduction last night, and from the darkening of his irises, she knew his did as well.

He took a sip of the bubbling, pale liquid. "I can't argue with results like yours." Before she drew her glass to her lips, he stopped her hand and led her a few steps to the left, away from the doorway and out of earshot of those standing nearby. He raised his glass an inch or so in a toast. "Here's to getting what we want."

Thick with the promise of passion, his whispered wish foreshadowed an evening of loving to match and surpass what they'd shared the night before. Maybe he'd forgotten his promise to take her to Moana's apartment after the wedding, but Harley hadn't. She suspected after that visit, she might never find herself the object of Grant's desires again. "What if what we want isn't what's best?"

He touched the base of her glass with one finger, then lifted until she took another sip. "I'm tired of playing 'what if.' I'd much rather play 'why not.'"

Her sip turned into a generous swallow, and in moments, she'd drained the champagne from her glass. Almost immediately, her skin warmed and her eyelids fluttered. Grant laughed and threw back his drink as well.

Taking her glass, he set the empty flutes on a passing waiter's tray and then hooked her hand in his arm once again. Wordlessly, he led her straight toward Mr. Phipps, whose party now included Grant's friend Mac and a stunning redhead who nervously nursed a club soda with lime.

"Ah, Grant. You look handsome, my boy. Very dapper." Howell Phipps grabbed Grant's hand nearly before he had a chance to offer it. "A great representative for First Investment, don't you agree, Amelia?"

Mrs. Phipps tore her appraising gaze away from Harley long enough to bestow Grant with a smile. "I'd trust you with my money."

Grant shook the woman's hand politely. "You already do, Mrs. Phipps. May I introduce Ms. Harley Monroe? Harley, this is Amelia and Howell Phipps."

Harley shook both their hands in turn, making sure to intensify her grip when Mrs. Phipps accepted her gesture. Something about the woman's cold gray stare made the hair on the back of her neck stand on end. She sought to unnerve Harley, put her on the defensive— and the feeling was eerily familiar.

"It's a pleasure to meet both of you," Harley said. "Grant speaks so highly of you both."

Mr. Phipps grinned and waved over a waiter with

another silver platter of champagne. From the gregari-
ousness of his manner and the nearly imperceptible
slur to his words, Harley knew he'd already had his
share of bubbly. "And we of him. He's a fine CEO. An
instinct for making money like I've never seen."

"And for choosing lovely women." Amelia took a
glass from the platter, but made no move to drink.
"Tell me, Ms. Monroe, where did you and Grant meet?
You're not from Citrus Hill."

Harley swallowed deeply, allowing Grant to beat
her to the explanation. "Harley's family. Distantly related. She's visiting the area for a few days."

Mrs. Phipps nodded and grinned, but Harley didn't
buy her easy acceptance one iota. Yet before the older
woman could form more probing questions, Grant began introducing her to the others in the party.

"You already know Mac. This is Mac's better half,
Jenna Malone."

Finally, a truly friendly face. Jenna's green eyes, a
perfect accompaniment to her flaming red hair, were
large and round and welcoming. The anxiety Harley
noted in her moments before seemed to disperse the
minute Harley stepped closer to her and extended her
hand. "Nice to meet you."

"Same here. More than you know."

Jenna glanced at Mrs. Phipps and Mrs. Ford furtively, leaving no question about her discomfort in
such upper-crust company. "Your dress is stunning.
Mac said the cab company that brought you to Grant's
lost your luggage. I figured that's why you didn't come
to the rehearsal."

She didn't know where Jenna had heard the story,
but the reference gave Harley a chance to chat confidently about the recent past, thus avoiding the blanks

in her memory and the lies she'd have to tell if Mrs. Phipps questioned her further.

"Grant picked this up for me in Tampa this morning. I wasn't prepared to attend something so formal."

Jenna sipped her soda and glanced sidelong at the crowd around them. "Well, I for one am glad you came. I didn't want to be the only stranger here."

Her words were a whisper, but Harley could hear her loud and clear. She said "stranger," but meant "outsider." Though Jenna dazzled with a beauty well beyond most of the glitterati around them, Harley sensed the woman's strong distaste for overdone wealth and pretentiousness. Her roots undoubtedly stemmed from a field more like Harley's—wide open, richly soiled, but a bit overgrown—and not the least like Grant's neatly rowed, carefully trimmed tillage of wealth and privilege.

Harley slipped her hand on Jenna's arm. "I know exactly what you mean."

Jenna's eyes darted to her husband and Grant, who discussed an upcoming golf date with Phipps and Bailey Ford. Their wives spoke in hushed tones, marveling at the expense and obvious taste in the floral arrangements and bridesmaids' dresses. While Harley agreed with the women's generous assessment, she felt neither qualified nor welcomed to comment.

"So," Jenna remarked, a wry twist to her voice, "how 'bout those Cleveland Indians?"

Harley laughed, uncertain why the offbeat comment amused her, but certain she liked Jenna Malone. The tension tightening her stomach muscles eased. If she stuck close to Mac's wife, she'd make it through the evening just fine.

Unfortunately, her confidence was short-lived. When the wedding coordinator bounced over to shoo them to their respective tables, Harley caught a glimpse of a blue-haired matron in a smart, satin-trimmed, silver-gray suit.

Wilhelmina Langley.

"We're sitting at one of the head tables," Grant informed Harley as he cupped her elbow and led her through the shifting crowd. Mac and Jenna followed close behind.

"In front of everyone?" She gulped audibly.

"It'll be fun," Grant promised. "This crowd isn't used to seeing me with a date. Everyone will wonder who you are."

"Not everyone."

She tilted her head sideways, enough for Grant to catch her hint and follow her gaze as it darted from him to Langley. Within moments, the seasoned columnist had them in her sight. She instantly detached herself from the people she spoke to and headed straight toward them.

"Well, Mr. Riordan, it's nice to see you've ended your self-imposed ban on bringing an escort to one of our events," she noted, sounding as if she owned the Citrus Hill social scene personally. Which in a way, she did.

"I thought I'd end the speculation."

Grant's words were cryptic, but Mrs. Langley seemed to interpret them with ease.

"End it? Dear boy, having such a lovely young lady on your arm will only fuel it. Luckily for you, I already know all about her. I should be able to quell any wild rumors before they cause any trouble."

"Quell the rumors? That will be a change for you."

Harley winced, but Mrs. Langley laughed out loud. "I suppose it will. We all need a change. Keeps us young. Harley, you look radiant."

Harley didn't quite know how to respond. She sensed shrewdness in Mrs. Langley's interaction with Grant, as if she owned a powerful secret about him—as if she knew the truth about Harley. Would Mrs. Langley's column tomorrow morning contain some scandalous hint of impropriety, or had the older woman dug straight through to the sordid facts?

"Thank you, Mrs. Langley. Do you know the Malones?"

Mrs. Langley greeted Jenna with a graciousness that belied her dominant position in the Citrus Hill social hierarchy. She asked Mac a few pointed questions regarding a recent police scandal in his jurisdiction, then returned her attention to Harley and Grant.

"I hope the two of you have a lovely evening."

Innocuous though the comment seemed, Harley couldn't help hearing the unsaid portion. *I hope the two of you have a lovely evening. Tomorrow might not be so enjoyable.*

Grant tugged on Harley's arm, reeling her even closer. "I can't see how I couldn't, considering the company I'm keeping."

Mrs. Langley's eyebrows rose just a fraction, then her smile deepened. But before Harley could determine the meaning of her abstract grin, Grant escorted her away.

Harley glanced over her shoulder as they wove through linen-covered tables bedecked with sparkling crystal and fine china. "Do you think that was wise, baiting her like that?"

Grant shrugged and slid out Harley's chair. "What have we got to lose? She may just think we're kissing cousins."

"You say that as if it's a good thing."

He eased into the seat beside her. "Depends on the cousin."

Mac and Jenna sat beside them on Harley's side, joined not too long after by Gus, his live-in, Lisa, and Grant's other friend, Mike and his date. Minutes later, the band leader announced the arrival of the bride and groom. They made their way through the crowd, danced their first dance to a Whitney Houston tune, then followed the wedding coordinator to a private table set upon a dais at the front of the hall.

"Mandy looks downright smitten," Harley commented. "Steve's one lucky man."

"I know how he feels," Grant said.

Harley leaned in closer, hoping her voice wouldn't carry. "You're awfully optimistic tonight. Yesterday, you were convinced Mrs. Langley knew everything and meant to expose you in tomorrow's edition."

With a confident snap, Grant flattened his swan-shaped napkin and laid it across his lap. Yesterday, the world had looked considerably bleaker. Darker. Colder. Like the life he'd grown so accustomed to. Since his night with Harley, the situation didn't seem so dire. Even if Langley did destroy his career, he'd survive. So would Nanna Lil. He was too busy enjoying his newfound freedom to concern himself with social politics.

And with Harley, creativity became second nature.

"Maybe she will. But let's not worry about that tonight." A waiter brought them cool glasses of white wine and served the salad of assorted bitter greens. "Eat your gourmet rabbit food and enjoy the atmosphere. I intend to burn a lot of calories later."

Harley speared an artichoke heart with her fork. "You dance?"

Grant dusted fresh pepper over the salad dressing. "Dance? I guess that burns calories too, doesn't it?"

His counterfeit attempt at innocence nearly caused Harley to choke on her endive. She swallowed a generous mouthful of wine, then smiled at Jenna, who eyed Harley and Grant suspiciously, then threw a surprised look at her husband. Mac nodded sagely. Harley's skin flushed.

The dinner conversation livened as the courses passed, with occasional breaks as guests tapped the crystal stemware, demanding the bride and groom kiss. Following the show of affection, the hall rang with surprisingly rowdy applause. The twelve-piece band slowly picked up the tempo of their music, and couple after couple left their chateaubriand to take a whirl on the parquet dance floor.

Slowly, the mood shifted from snobbish pretense to genuine glee. Though Harley suspected the change stemmed from the open bar and free-flowing wine, she appreciated the transformation. In such an atmosphere, she didn't care who saw Grant lay his hand protectively on her arm during dessert or lift his napkin to wipe away a dollop of whipped cream clinging to her lips just before cordials arrived at the table.

Harley eyed her snifter longingly, but felt sure she couldn't force another morsel of food or drink into her mouth.

"Don't you like brandy?" Grant raised his glass to her in a tiny toast.

"I don't have room to find out. I think I overindulged." She pushed the remnants of her raspberry chocolate torte further away.

Grant's smirk revealed the artful naughtiness he'd practiced on her all night long. "There are good things to be said for overindulgence."

Harley slipped her napkin off her lap. "Not if I don't want this dress to rip at the seams."

"There are good things to be said for that, too."

She rolled her eyes for effect, but secretly, her insides curled and constricted. Grant's flirtation since his return from the tuxedo shop this morning had been nearly nonstop. She wanted nothing more than to go home and make love with him after the wedding, which as Mandy promised, invoked romance and spirited expectation in every candelabra, every musical selection, every wisp of soft bridal satin.

Instead, she asked Jenna for the time.

"Nearly seven. It's early yet. Ask Grant to dance. I bet I can coerce Mac onto the floor if Grant goes first."

The band's blithe rhythms had enticed Harley all night. She'd worked to keep her shoulders still and her hips firmly planted in her chair, especially after the band abandoned the subtle dinner music in favor of more lively tunes. When the percussionist began beating a Latin tempo, Harley could resist no longer.

"Can you tango?"

Grant's brown eyes bulged. "Not since my last cotillion. I was all of fourteen and not very coordinated."

She grabbed his hand. "Trust me, your coordination has improved. Let's dance."

Half expecting Grant to pull her back into her chair, Harley stood and turned to the dance floor. Surprisingly, Grant followed close behind. Couples ranging in age from midtwenties to late seventies filled in the spaces around them, forcing Grant and Harley to stand close.

Lights muted by red-and-purple gels cast a risqué glow, enhancing the music's hypnotic rhythm. Some dancers continued to waltz stiffly. Others paced the length of the floor crouched low with clenched hands extended, practically begging for someone to toss them a rose to clamp between their teeth.

Harley, on the other hand, felt compelled to rise on the balls of her feet and swing her arm carelessly over Grant's shoulder. She hooked one ankle around his calf. Their noses touched. His breath flushed her lips with heat. When he smoothed his hand down her side, his palm hot against the cool silk, she arched her back. Grant braced her with a hand firmly between her shoulder blades, dipping her backward then easing her up until they again stood face to face.

She knew this dance. Without thought, her feet moved. Without planning, her body swayed and spun. Grant held her close, his eyes cast down as he followed her lead. The rhythm they'd found in lovemaking matched the cadence of the dance. In moments, they rediscovered the scorching tempo.

Harley pulled her breath from deep within, burning a path to her lungs. Lightheadedness battled with her balance. Only mildly aware of the sea of eyes assessing them, the dance elicited a freedom of movement that unburdened her steps. Grant's steadying hand and locked gaze kept her anchored. If he released her, she felt sure she'd float away.

When she lunged away from him, he yanked her back, slamming her against his rock-hard chest. His heart pounded like a steel drum. They stilled, then swayed, then spun madly until an intrinsic burst of joy bubbled from within her into a devilish laugh.

The music ended and the crowd's applause slowly brought her back from the dream the tango wove. Grant, still clutching her close, neither smiled nor frowned. His expression reflected utter fascination.

"You're amazing."

She lowered her lashes, attempting to hide the scarlet flush tinting her face. "I don't know where that came from. I don't remember ever..."

And yet she did. While the band struck up a cover of a popular disco tune, Harley remembered dancing the tango in a room full of people, remembered being the center of attention, remembered despising the man who led her in the dance—a man whose face remained vague and insubstantial.

The memory bore little resemblance to her tango with Grant. In her past, she sensed dancing had been a chore—a job with counted-out steps and carefully timed pivots and dips. With Grant, music and emotions guided her, filling her with a pulse equal to her most sensuous desires.

Grant took her hand and led her from the dance floor. "You're an amazing dancer. I just can't believe..."

He stopped midsentence, causing Harley to set her memory aside. "Can't believe what?" Her chest constricted with mild indignation. "That my dancing doesn't always entail the removal of my clothes?"

He pulled her closer and whispered into her ear. "Honey, if you dance that way when we're alone, I can guarantee there won't be a stitch left on you."

She pushed away lightly, slightly chagrined. "I don't know what came over me. I'm sorry if I embarrassed you."

"Embarrassed me?" Grant's bright-eyed gaze testified to his disbelief. Just as quickly, his irises darkened to their richest shade of brown. He wrapped his hands around her waist, allowing his fingers to dip just low enough to remain innocent, while reminding her of how he adored her bottom. "There wasn't a woman in this room who didn't want to be you just then. Or a man who didn't want to be your partner."

Grabbing his hands and placing them firmly on her waist alone, she squirmed away a few inches, clipped a lock of hair behind her ear and darted her gaze over her shoulder. "Someone might see. It's bad enough I did the Dance of the Seven Veils out there."

Grant licked his lips and wished Harley hadn't chosen that particular metaphor. The image of her dancing and shedding translucent scarves until she stood naked and glorious before him came all too easily. He knew for a fact he didn't have anything remotely resembling a veil at the house, and couldn't think of a single place to buy any on their way home.

Except they wouldn't be going straight home. She'd told him on the way to the wedding about her plan to go to Moana's apartment at nine o'clock. He checked his watch. Ten after seven.

The night was still young.

He crooked his finger beneath her chin and fought the urge to kiss her silly. "If that tango was any indication, I'm taking a rain check on a real veil dance, sweetheart. But now, I think I'd better see how the wedding is progressing. We can't leave until they throw the bouquet and we'll need at least a half hour to make it to Tampa. Why don't I go see if I can hurry things along?"

Harley nodded and he led her back to the table without another word. Jenna, who sat alone nursing her coffee, immediately brightened when Harley approached. He left them chatting about Harley's dance talent and went in search of the groom.

He found Mac instead.

"Where've you been?"

Mac shoved his cell phone back in his pocket. "Checking with the precinct. I don't have to ask you that question. A few minutes ago, a gang of juvies could have lifted every purse and wallet in the place and no one would've noticed. Is there something between you and our mystery woman that you aren't telling me?"

Grant combed his fingers through his hair. "Yes."

Mac waited expectantly, then chuckled when Grant's lips remained closed. "I get the hint. In case you're interested, she's still not listed as missing. And that address you got for the other stripper—very ritzy. I know exotic dancers make good money, but to afford Davis Island, I think they'd have to have some…more lucrative…business on the side."

Grant ground his teeth at Mac's implication. "I don't think Harley…"

Mac held his hands up in instant surrender. "I didn't say a thing about Harley. She seems, I don't know, classy. Besides, a girl doesn't learn to move like that on street corners or strip joints."

Admittedly, neither man knew much about dancing, but Grant had attended enough cotillions, balls and benefits to know a trained dancer when he saw one. Or better yet, danced with one. And while parents of all financial backgrounds enrolled their daughters in ballet, not too many other than the wealthy or socially ambitious opted for ballroom instruction.

Another clue to add to the mystery that was Harley.

Yet for now, her safety was his prime concern. "You think Moana is into something illegal to afford her high-class address?"

Mac shrugged. "Either her or her boyfriend. Or both. What was his name? Maybe I know him."

Grant searched his memory for the name, knowing Joy had mentioned it at the strip club. "I didn't listen closely to that part. Chuck or something. She said he was a real sleaze. Had some goons after him."

Searching through the crowd, Mac waved at Jenna and Harley. "Look, let me take Jenna home and then I'll go with you to Moana's place. Maybe Harley will stay with her and we can…"

Grant shook his head. Keenly aware of how little attention Mac paid to his lovely new wife, he wouldn't be the cause of more strife between them. Besides, he'd gotten to know Harley incredibly well in the last two days. He couldn't imagine her willingly staying behind. "Harley's got quite an independent streak. You stay here and dance with your wife. I'll take care of Harley."

Mac nodded, somewhat repentantly, slapped Grant on the shoulder and headed back to the table.

Grant scanned the crowd for Steve and Mandy, then checked his watch again and wondered if he'd made the right choice to decline Mac's offer. An odd rumble trembled in his gut—a cross between an ulcer and a warning of danger. He couldn't fathom exposing Harley to a perilous situation, even if the outcome might cure her amnesia.

He wondered, though, if he'd have any choice—if he'd ever had any choice—or if he ever would again. Harley managed him with the same skill he used on his client's investments. And, sometimes, he was sure she wasn't even trying. Still, he surrendered to her voluntarily, with eager anticipation and total trust, completely contrary to how he'd behaved in his recent past as a world-class control freak.

And yet, even she couldn't derail his vow to protect her from anyone or anything aiming to hinder her invigorating spirit—Moana's seedy troubles, Mrs. Langley's poison pen, her uncertain past, or Howell Phipps.

Grant groaned when he spotted his boss making a determined beeline toward him. Straightening his jacket, he steeled himself for the chastising he was undoubtedly about to receive. Grim lines marred the older man's already wrinkled face. A frown made his jowls seem as large as a hound dog's.

"I hope you're pleased with that little performance."

Not a bad opening. Relatively benign in comparison to Phipps' usual rants.

Grant cracked an irreverent grin. "I am. I always thought I had two left feet."

Phipps grabbed Grant's arm and led him from earshot of other guests. "Now isn't the time for becoming a smartass, Riordan. Your display on the dance floor bordered on shameful. You may enjoy the wagging tongues, but I find it tiresome. And don't for one minute think I believe Miss Monroe is related to you. I don't know who she is, but if she's anything short of saintly, I'll..."

Grant tugged his arm away and shoved his hands in his pockets. The temptation to punch Phipps squarely in his arrogant face nearly overrode his self-control. "You'll what? You'll fire me? Since I've taken over First Investment, your profits have soared. Investors by the dozens have joined the firm. You can't afford to lose me."

Phipps's eyes narrowed as a red flush spread from neck to cheeks to forehead. "No, I can't. But you can't afford to lose your position, either. I know your situation. If I have a mind to, I can ensure that no investor in the entire southeast will give you one red cent to work with. I value your contribution to the firm, Riordan, but I'll not have another spectacle on my hands. I won't let another horny CEO bring my firm down."

Though the threat was real, Grant wouldn't allow himself to be bullied. "I'm the best thing that's happened to this company in a long time." He pressed a pointed finger into Phipps's chest. "If you plan to force me out, you'd better have something on me a lot stronger than a sensual dance with a beautiful woman. A woman, by the way, whom I respect immensely."

Phipps backed up a step and straightened the front of his shirt. "If she's not worthy of that respect in the least little way, I'll have all I need. Maybe you don't give a damn about yourself, but what about her? Do you think she'd enjoy being the object of very public scrutiny? Think about that."

Howell Phipps turned brusquely away and headed back into the reception. If not for the crowd, Grant would have put a fist through the richly papered wall. Phipps didn't make threats he didn't intend to follow through on, and Grant knew that first thing Monday morning, a private investigator would begin sorting through Harley's past. Notwithstanding the danger to his own career, the embarrassment to Harley could be devastating. She didn't deserve public ridicule or scorn like the greedy madam or indiscreet secretary involved in the previous First Investment scandals.

He had no credentials to make a professional call, but Grant acknowledged Harley's fragile psyche. Her inner confidence waned whenever she confronted the fact that she was a stripper. How would a front-page splash announcing her profession play in a mind already so damaged by some terrible event that she couldn't remember her true identity?

Grant raked his hands through his hair, tugging at his scalp as he imagined the potential devastation. No matter the cost to his personal life, he couldn't let Howell Phipps or anyone else hurt Harley. He stepped back into the hall, for a minute unable to find Harley at the table. Soon, the crowd parted enough for him to catch a glimpse of her ebony hair, bent near Jenna's upswept coif of burnished red. Chatting with his friends, she remained blissfully unaware of how he—the man she'd invested her entire trust in—could soon become the cause of her ultimate destruction.

"I'M GOING WITH YOU." Harley plucked the car door lock open manually, despite Grant's refusal to automatically unlock the door until she agreed to stay in the car.

"We don't know what to expect. You should wait until I check things out."

Harley's gaze impaled him with sharp anger. "This is my life. My memory. You've been a real prince up to now, Grant. Don't start playing tyrant."

He grabbed her hand before she slipped completely off the leather seat into the well-lit parking lot. Her fingers seemed small and delicate in his large palm, her eyes innocent, despite the intestinal fortitude she'd shown from the moment they met.

"I don't want anything bad to happen to you."

Her lips twisted into something he couldn't quite identify—not a smile, definitely, but not a grimace either. Something in between.

"Me neither. But we're so close. I won't turn back— or skulk in the shadows." She took one last glance at the address Joy had written. "Three-D. Come on. For all we know, Moana didn't get my message and isn't even back in town."

Grant released her, slid out of the Mercedes and engaged the alarm. Not that he suspected he'd need the extra security in this condominium complex. Despite Mac's warnings of possible criminal activity, tall, well-spaced palm trees and trimmed azalea bushes gave the high-rise the air of a vacation resort rather than a residence. Bright pink lamps, reminiscent of antique fixtures, lit the spacious parking lot. Smaller lights plugged into the thick green lawn bathed the sidewalks in sharp amber. The condominium's entrance, with double sliding glass doors and a manned security window, further convinced Grant that he'd let his imagination run rampant.

He pulled Harley aside as a large group of people, a diverse crowd judging from the ages and manners of dress, came up from behind. He and Harley turned down no less than three invitations to the party on the eighth floor.

"Why don't you talk to the guard?" Grant suggested. "He might recognize you."

Harley eyed him doubtfully.

"You never know."

She shrugged, put on her best smile, and knocked lightly on the window with her knuckle.

"Ms. Roberts! Haven't seen you around for a couple of days. I thought maybe you and your cousin'd gone back to Miami."

Harley glanced nervously at Grant, but kept her smile fixed. "I just went to Citrus Hill for a few days. Is Moa...my cousin...home? I called and told her I was coming in tonight."

The guard's rounded face twisted in thought. "I haven't seen her since Thursday. She left a key for you." He dug around beneath the counter, grinning ear-to-ear when he produced the silver key dangling from a heart-shaped ring. He slid it through a slot between the glass and the countertop.

Harley looked at the key briefly, then clutched it in her palm. "But she's not back?"

The disappointment in her voice was impossible to hide.

"She could've come here earlier. I just started my

shift and I've had crowds coming in nonstop for the party in 8-A. Let me call up."

When he turned around to dial his house phone, Harley mouthed the word "cousin" to Grant with a hopeful smile. He patted her softly on the shoulder. So she was the family Joy said Moana regretted leaving behind in Miami. He understood the sentiment perfectly.

"Yes, ma'am. I'll buzz her in." The guard pressed a button somewhere below the window. "Go on up. She sounds sleepy." He hung up the phone and winced. "I think I woke her up."

"I'm sure she'll forgive you."

Harley slipped the key into her purse and moved to the door quickly. Grant watched her hand shake as she set it on the latch and pulled forward. Once out of earshot of the guard, she whispered gleefully to Grant, "I'm from Miami. My last name is Roberts."

Grant fought the urge to take her hand in his and keep her from pressing the elevator button. Suddenly, the notion of discovering her past didn't seem so cut and dried.

"I heard."

Her gaze assessed him sharply, and he was careful to sustain his supportive grin until the elevator dinged and distracted her attention.

"Harley Roberts. Harley Roberts." She pressed the button for the third floor and closed her eyes, repeating the name with conviction, then trying to hide her disappointment when the name remained hollow and empty. "Maybe seeing Moana will help."

"Maybe."

Grant leaned back against the polished brass elevator wall and dug his hands deep into his tuxedo pockets. Words swam in a jumble of mixed thoughts and wishes. He wanted to tell her that her past didn't matter to him—even if she did make a living taking her clothes off for other men. He wanted to assure her that neither her job nor her life-style could interfere with his professional needs and personal goals. He wanted to promise he'd never let his close-minded boss put her up to public scorn.

Yet the words wouldn't come. He contemplated his shoes instead of sharing in Harley's expectant impatience. So close now to filling in the blanks left by her accident, he wasn't sure which, if any, of those assertions were true.

The elevator slowed, then stilled. The doors swished open and Harley bit her lip. "Well, this is it. Harley Roberts," she spoke into the empty hallway, "this is your life."

She stepped off the elevator confidently. Grant hesitated. He didn't want to know who Harley'd been before she tumbled into his life. He knew that now. She barreled forward as if world peace hinged on her discoveries. He lingered behind.

The elevator doors started sliding back together. Grant shot forward, trying to block the mechanism from closing, but a meaty fist, attached to an equally beefy face and body, caught his hand like an underhanded pitch and threw him backward.

"You're going down, asshole."

Harley screamed, spurring Grant to regain his balance. He braced both hands between the closing doors and pressed outward. His reward was a kick to the abdomen that sent him flying into the back wall.

His attacker, his hair a matted blond and his eyes red-rimmed and glossy, stepped onto the elevator and grinned. "Now, we're gonna have some fun."

10

ONE CALLUSED HAND clamped over her mouth, stopping her midscream, while a second bit into her bare wrists, clenching her arms together like handcuffs in one thick paw. Her eyes watered in pain and fear. Who was this man? What did he want with her? Had he or his ally hurt Grant? She struggled against the bruising agony, trying to recapture her balance, fighting to yell for help. Without loosening his hold, he shoved her forward.

"Quit fighting and keep quiet. Just gotta ask you a question. Nothing to be afraid of."

His tone contained a hint of laughter. Her skin rippled with gooseflesh. His breath, humid against her neck, reeked of raw tobacco—the type men chomped on for hours, then spit out wherever and whenever it suited them. Her stomach roiled and she fought the urge to gag. Then again, maybe if she vomited, he'd let her go and she could escape.

But to where? Nothing down this hall but four doors generously spread apart and marked for condominiums A through D.

The door to Moana's condo, the last in the hall, stood ajar. He pushed her inside, pausing until his companion entered, closed and bolted the door behind him. He released her arms, but kept his hand firmly over her mouth.

"Sit. One peep and I'll get mad. You won't like me if I'm mad. Understand?"

Harley hesitated, trying to remember what the self-defense experts said about screaming. Should she obey his order or defy him? She remembered she wasn't supposed to get in a car with a kidnapper. Never get in the car. Right. But if she screamed? Even if someone heard her, what would they do? Ignore her? Call security? Call the police? The door was dead-bolted. Endless, painful minutes could pass before anyone could come to her aid.

She nodded compliantly.

"Good girl." He released her by propelling her onto a sage-green leather couch. "Stay put till I'm ready for you."

She braced her fall with her hands, but still landed face down and skirt up. Though she twisted quickly to cover herself, she heard the spine-curdling sound of the other man's lecherous whistle.

Grant, where are you?

GRANT SLAMMED HIS FIST into his attacker's face with the full force of a power driver. The first four punches were for Harley. The fifth and sixth repaid the scum for Grant's aching gut. By the time the street tough lay unconscious on the elevator floor, Grant had made the man pay for every single instance when he had held back or remained calm, professional and detached. The thug had picked the wrong night to mess with Grant Riordan. Pain shot through his arm. His fist was bloodied and sore. His lungs burned with each ragged breath.

He'd never felt better in his life.

When the elevator finally stopped, he squeezed between the spreading doors into the lobby, dragging the unconscious criminal by the collar. He tossed him against the glass partition and banged twice to alert the security guard.

"Call the police. There's trouble on the third floor."

The friendly guard's face turned ashen white. He hesitated, then fumbled for his standard issue revolver. "Who's that?"

Grant was already halfway across the lobby. He didn't need this well-meaning, but reluctant cop-wannabe putting Harley's life in danger. He'd done that well enough on his own.

"He jumped me. Keep him there until the cops come."

"I should go!" The portly guard struggled, but finally managed to open the door from his station.

"No. Guard the perp. I'm a cop."

The lie rolled off his tongue with the same speed as his feet up the stairs. After passing the second floor landing, he slowed to quiet his steps. All he had on his side was the element of surprise.

The hall outside the stairs echoed with eerie silence. His back to the wall, he inched down the corridor. He had no doubt they'd taken Harley into Moana's condo. More than likely, Harley's kidnappers were the same thugs Joy told them were looking for Moana and her creep of a boyfriend. They must have gotten into the building with the crowds attending the party upstairs, broken into the apartment, heard Harley's message announcing the time of her arrival and been lying in wait.

When and if he ever found Moana's boyfriend, he was going to kill him. But first, he could only concern himself with formulating a plan. He'd have a better chance of snatching Harley away if he could draw the kidnappers out of the condo. Best scenario would be leading them downstairs to the police—or at least, the armed guard.

Since First Financial also housed a full service bank, all employees had been trained how to react in a robbery situation. *Give them what they want* had been the mantra of security experts and police alike. No amount of cash could be worth the price of someone's life.

But these people hadn't taken something as unimportant or as easily replaceable as cash. They'd taken the woman who'd made him feel alive for the first time in his life—the woman he was falling in love with. And when he leaned his ear to the door of apartment 3-D and heard nothing but muffled voices—none of which sounded like Harley—another thought occurred to him. These goons didn't want Harley either. They wanted Moana's boyfriend.

So he'd just have to give them what they wanted.

KEEPING HER EYES downcast, Harley listened as her captor rifled through the drawers and closets of the adjacent room, speaking in quiet tones to someone she couldn't see. The whistler stayed near the door. Furtively, Harley glanced around, testing her recognition of Moana's apartment while remaining careful not to look up. Maybe if they thought she couldn't identify them, they'd find no reason to hurt her.

The furnishings and floor plan were as foreign as the man who dragged her inside. She steadied her breathing, focusing solely on connecting some object to her own past. If these men wanted to ask her questions, the queries wouldn't deal with the last two days in Citrus Hill. They'd want to know about Moana, about her boyfriend, about the part of Harley's life she couldn't recall—the part Grant's boss threatened to expose if he didn't watch his step.

At the wedding, she hadn't wanted to eavesdrop. Telling herself she'd only search for the bathroom, she'd followed Grant the minute she saw Howell Phipps grab his arm and lead him from the reception. Just as she'd feared, her presence and disreputable behavior had caused Grant undeserved trouble with his boss.

And now, she could have cost him his health, maybe even his life.

You're going down. She'd barely heard the threat under her own captured scream, but she'd known the instant the elevator doors whooshed shut that she couldn't help Grant any more than he could help her. For all she knew, a third man, maybe a fourth, jumped into the elevator before it descended, specifically to ensure Grant didn't interfere with her interrogation.

And what about Moana? Was she here? Was she hurt?

A pair of high-heeled, ankle-length boots stepped in front of her. Moana?

"Give it up, Tower. Ain't nothing in there. Check the back closet again."

The woman's lazy drawl and guttural delivery rang no bell of recognition.

"You can look at me, angel-face. We want you to tell that double-crossin' creep Buck exactly who's looking for 'im."

Harley's gaze panned up, taking in the woman's stick-thin legs ensconced in black mesh stockings, cut-off black denim hip-hugging shorts and frazzled halter top. Her makeup, boldly applied, favored black in everything from lipstick to eyeliner—straight to the roots of her frosted blond hair. She appeared better suited for Halloween or a biker bar than breaking and entering. Especially if she didn't want to be noticed.

This definitely wasn't Moana, though she'd obviously impersonated her when the guard had called. Joy's comment at the strip club about "biker-chick" regalia not being Moana's style lingered in Harley's brain.

"I don't know Buck," Harley said, thrusting her chin up in a manner she hoped would denote courage, but not defiance. She braced both feet firmly on the carpeted floor, preparing to bolt at her first opportunity.

The woman smoothed her hands over her nearly nonexistent hips and lifted her booted foot onto the lacquered coffee table. "I'm surprised. He's just the type to salivate over a sweet little thing like you." She leaned her elbow on her knee, and slipped a short-handled knife out of her boot.

Harley ignored the unsheathed blade. "He sounds like a real winner."

The woman's laugh was raspy, but genuine. Her ample breasts jiggled, revealing the absence of a bra. "Buck couldn't win a one-man boxing match. Not after what he's pulled."

Harley kept her stare steady, letting the woman know she couldn't care less about what happened to the cretin they searched for. She felt nothing for this Buck person, except a lingering dislike that could have stemmed either from her past or from the fact that he was the reason these hoodlums had attacked Grant and detained her. "Look, I don't know Buck and I don't know where he is. I can't help you, so why don't you just let me leave and we'll forget all about this?"

Judiciously, she made no move to depart.

"I wish it was so easy, angel-face. See, my old man wants to 'talk' to Buck. Real bad. Seems some money's missing from his last shipment. And I ain't talkin' pennies. Me and my pals been hanging out in Tampa a week trying to find the snake. I'm sick of this town, but I can't go back empty-handed."

Harley heard the subtle threat, but bit the inside of her bottom lip to stop herself from reacting in any way that might appear threatening or antagonistic. The woman still kept the blade folded into the ivory handle. Harley didn't want that to change.

"I'm not worth your time," Harley noted.

"Ah, but you know Buck's girlfriend, Moana." The woman grabbed an acrylic-framed picture from the coffee table and turned it so Harley could see the snapshot. Three smiling faces, two teenage girls and a toddler, flashed goofy grins at the camera. "You're the brunette. And yours is the voice on her answering machine."

Harley yearned to examine the photo more closely, but preferred to remain at arm's distance. Still, she could see herself clearly in the dark-haired girl's fresh face. The teen she assumed was Moana, red-haired and a little older, displayed a grin that didn't quite reach her eyes. With a mouth rimmed by the ice cream he held between two pudgy hands, the child fairly bubbled with carefree mirth.

And in the background, Harley clearly saw the outline of a pink stucco house. The same one from her dream.

"I've been looking for Moana for three days. I left the message hoping she'd retrieve it from wherever she was and meet me tonight."

"Three days is a long time. Why'd you only leave a message this morning?"

"I got desperate. I need to talk to her, but for entirely different reasons than yours."

Her captor's eye's narrowed. "What kind of reasons?"

Harley's attention returned to the photograph. "Family matters. Nothing you'd care about."

The woman nodded slowly and slapped the blade's handle in her palm, as if mulling over Harley's explanation. When one of her companions, the medium-built grease-head with the wolfish whistle, slid back to lean his ear against the front door, the woman's sharp gaze darted away.

"Tower, come out here," she called, her voice a hissing whisper.

The giant who'd snared Harley in the hallway emerged from the other room. A jagged scar, still puffed and red as if newly attained, ran the length of his face from forehead to chin, splitting his face into two halves, one as frightening as the other. "Yeah, Riva?"

Riva crooked her head toward the door. The tall, bulky man slid his hand into his jacket. Harley froze. When his hand emerged, he'd slid a four-fingered metal ring over his knuckles. No gun. Harley blew out a breath, then scooted forward, prepared to either run or hide as necessary.

"Hang tight, angel-face," Riva commented, unfolding her knife. "You're not going anywhere."

Harley held her hands up in surrender. "No problem."

From the other side of the door, Harley heard a man's voice. "Dammit. Where the hell are my keys?"

Wolf-whistle pulled out his own knife and motioned for the thug called Tower to give him space. He complied after Riva nodded her agreement.

"Moana, get your ass in gear! I can't find my damn keys."

Riva's ebony lips stretched into a satisfied smile. She

undoubtedly expected the voice on the other side of the door to belong to the elusive Buck.

Harley knew differently. She'd know Grant's voice anywhere. Despite his attempt to sound like a street tough, the distinct rhythm of refinement clung to the edge of his tone.

Her heart soared for an instant, then halted mid-flight. What did he think he was doing? These criminals wanted Buck for nefarious reasons. Grant had levied himself in the middle of an ugly situation, at best. As intimidating as he was in the world of high finance, Riva and her boys didn't look like they'd give a flip about that kind of power. Harley's mind flashed pictures of Tower's brass-enhanced fists turning Grant's gorgeous face into bloody pulp. She imagined the shorter guy whistling an upbeat tune while he carved into Grant's muscled chest.

All because of her and her questionable past.

"What do you mean you left your purse in the car?"

Grant let loose a string of curses that would make any back-alley resident prouder than punch. When Harley heard his voice recede down the hall, she didn't know whether to be relieved or distressed.

He was leaving.

She swallowed deeply, then watched Wolf-whistle grasp the doorknob.

"Damn." Riva seemed to forget Harley in her rush to the door. "Don't let that bastard slip away. Go after him."

Grant was drawing them away.

"Bring him back here?"

Riva glanced around at the rifled condo, ignoring Harley altogether. "What the hell for? Let's jump the jerk and blow this joint."

Without another word, all three left, leaving the door

open behind them. Harley sat perfectly still, fearing her movement would cause them to return and take her hostage again. She heard them swear when they reached the corridor near the elevator.

Grant had escaped.

The door to the stairwell banged open just as the second elevator dinged its arrival.

Moments later, silence began to calm Harley's pounding heart. Grant had bought her an opportunity to flee. After a quick look around the apartment, she grabbed the picture from the coffee table and barreled to the door.

Straight into Grant's waiting arms.

He covered her mouth with his hand, quelling her startled scream.

"Hush, honey, it's me."

Despite his tight embrace and soothing tone, her entire frame shook. Tears of relief pooled at the edge of her lashes. He removed his palm from her lips, smoothing his warm touch beneath her chin.

"How did you…?" Each word left her mouth in a stilted squeak. "Your hand…"

"Shh. I'm fine. I rang for the elevator and hid in the stairwell until they went down. They're going to find the police downstairs, not Buck. Are you all right? They didn't hurt you, did they?"

Harley heard the tortured anxiety in his voice and knew she couldn't tell him about her sore wrists or aching jaw. Or the brandished knives. She didn't need him rushing to confront her captors, unleashing that wild part of him. She needed the untamed Grant here and now. Holding her. Driving her fears away.

"I'm fine. But the police? That'll get your name in the paper. Your boss…"

"We don't have to talk to the police. They'll detain

Moana's friends long enough for us to slip out. Now, let's get going. They could come back if they sense trouble. We'll take the stairs to that party on the eighth floor and wait until the coast is clear."

Grant wrapped his arm around her, checked the hall, then led her up the stairwell. She slipped her shoes off to move more freely and quietly. Grant took her spiky heels in one hand, grasping the thin straps between his strong fingers. The gesture, so obviously meaningless, made her want to cry.

Disco music and shouted conversations blared from apartment 8-A, and they blended in without drawing a single suspicious glance. Grant brought Harley a drink, but she waved it away, preferring to sit in a dimly lit corner and examine the photograph from Moana's apartment. She traced the round face of the toddler with a gentle finger. She knew those eyes. Big and blue and full of laughter. Suddenly, she caught the image of that same azure stare, only older, and not so brimming with happiness.

Instead, they were dark with worry. Disappointment.

Don't worry, Sammy. It won't be long. I'll be back for you before the end of the school year. I promise.

She remembered the pledge, but not the time or place or circumstances of her saying the words. She knew the child, now a teenager if her dream proved accurate, but she couldn't pinpoint their relationship. Was he a cousin like Moana? A brother? A friend?

Whoever he was, she'd spent her entire life caring for and protecting him. Somewhere, this boy waited for her—counted on her—to make good on her vow.

And she had no idea how to do that.

Her mind reeled. Hugging the picture tightly to her chest, she cursed her malfunctioning brain. Gus had told Grant that her amnesia probably stemmed from some trauma or group of traumas her conscious mind simply couldn't deal with. Was she still so weak that she couldn't face her troubles head on? She shook more violently in impotent frustration.

"Hey, we're safe." Grant spoke directly into her ear, rubbing her arms and back with gentle reassurance, completely unaware that her quaking stemmed from deeper fears. "No one's going to hurt you again. I promise."

His eyes, dark and determined, bored straight into her heart, touching her in a place that yearned to be touched, soothing her the way she needed to be soothed. He'd proven time and again that he'd endanger his career for her. And tonight, he'd risked both his professional position and his life.

She'd find a way to thank him before she left. To find Sammy. To find herself.

"I believe you, Grant. I always have."

After twenty minutes, they slipped out with a crowd heading to another celebration in a nearby building. With blue-and-red lights strobing the front entrance, Grant led Harley out the back and then around to his car. As they drove off, Harley saw her kidnappers leaning against a patrol car, being questioned by uniformed officers.

Grant left the radio off for the first part of their drive back to Citrus Hill. The silence soothed her frazzled nerves and allowed her to focus on devising a means to cure her amnesia. Tomorrow, she'd ask Gus about seeing a doctor who specialized in memory dysfunction. On the brink of regaining her past, Harley couldn't imagine continuing like this—remembering snippets and pieces of her life, but never the whole story, never the entire truth. She had no means to pay for the therapy, but she'd go back to stripping if she had to. No matter the price, she had to find the young boy who waited for her to come home.

Tonight, she'd say her goodbyes. Since the moment she'd first opened her eyes in Grant's living room, she knew she didn't belong there. She'd stayed out of desperation. Then out of desire. Now, no matter how much she loved Grant for jeopardizing his life and career for her, she had to clear out. Never mind Howell Phipps's not-so-subtle threats. So long as she remained protected in Grant's house and his embrace, her brain might never confront whatever tragedy kept her trapped in the amnesia.

Leaning forward, she clicked on the radio and tuned to a classical station that played jazz after hours. Grant reached out and captured her hand before she released the knob on the volume.

"You're still shaking." He threaded his fingers with hers, balancing their hands on the gearshift as they sped down the darkened interstate highway.

She fought to pull away, but she didn't want to let go. That was her problem. "I'll be fine."

He squeezed a little tighter. "You handled yourself damn well." Raising her knuckles to his mouth, he placed a soft kiss there, then clutched her hand to his heart.

The gesture nearly tore a sob from deep within her. The prospect of leaving him, of never seeing him again, shattered her from the inside out. One moment more, one caress more and she'd surely go insane. Carefully, she extracted her fingers from his.

"I just did what I had to."

Just as she had when she'd insinuated herself into Grant's life. And when she'd surrendered to him in his home gym. And when she fell in love with him. She'd had little choice in any of those actions, as much as she tried to believe otherwise.

Staying with Grant that first night kept her off the streets. Making love with him fed a ravenous hunger that threatened to consume her. Falling in love with him happened before she'd even realized.

But now, she had choices. She could ask Grant to further risk his career by helping her arrange her therapy. She could enlist his assistance in tracking down Sammy and Moana, even though doing so might endanger his life again.

Or she could leave in the morning. Venture out on her own. She knew her name now. Had a family tie. A hometown. Maybe later, after she'd reconstructed her memory and reestablished her life, she'd return and explore her feelings for Grant.

The realization ripped through her heart like a drill. In such a short time, she'd come to rely on his presence, come to lean on his strength. Yet she couldn't take the easy road any longer. To do so would put the man she loved at even further risk than she already had. No matter what trauma she'd experienced before this, nothing could compare to her being the cause of Grant's destruction. Nothing.

With her decision made, she leaned back into the car seat and watched the lighted billboards flash by until a sickening dizziness lured her to sleep.

"HARLEY, HON, WE'RE HOME."

Her lids fluttered opened and she glanced around, confused by the yawning iron gate and manicured lawn. Where was the gravel drive? The pink stucco? The flapping flag with the preening flamingo?

Reality dawned slowly. It wasn't her home he'd brought her to, but his. A place of taste and class and beauty, traits completely foreign to where she'd grown up. Her dream in the car was the same as the last. Of the house. The costumes. Sammy's metallic smile.

Grant pulled into the garage and turned off the engine.

"Are you all right?"

She straightened from her slumped position in the seat and unhooked her seat belt, stretching her arms and shoulders as freely as possible in Grant's compact luxury car. "I feel like I've been hit by a Mack truck."

Grant's grin nearly lightened her mood. "I have just the remedy."

The prospect of receiving another of Grant's massages perked her right up. She eagerly accepted his hand as he helped her from the car, then followed him inside wordlessly. He'd already told her about the box of condoms he'd purchased that morning, and since she feared this would be their last night together, she hoped to put each and every one to good use.

She slipped her jacket over a kitchen chair, then did the same with his. Kicking off her spiky heels, she leaned against the table while Grant perused the contents of his refrigerator.

"You too keyed up for wine?" he asked.

She rolled her neck in a semicircle, humming her approval at the liberating cracks and crunches. "Can you be too keyed up for wine?"

He grinned, pulled out a bottle of blush, shoved a corkscrew in his pocket, found two glasses in the cabinet, and with his hands full, extended his arm for Harley to tuck into as they left the dark kitchen.

She thought they'd go upstairs for their private interlude, but Grant led her to the pool area. He set the wine on the tiled table and disappeared into a shadowy corner while he fiddled with the light switches. In minutes, the entire patio, pool and bubbling hot tub rippled with soft blue light.

To Harley, the temperature on this sultry April night climbed a notch or two. "This is awfully romantic for a corporate mansion. Did one of the previous Don Juan-CEOs live here before you?"

He uncorked the bottle with little effort and poured her a generous portion. The glass immediately fogged with condensation. "I'm the first."

She accepted the wine with a skeptical smirk. "I find it hard to believe *you* had this lighting put in."

Taking a sip from his own glass, he sidled up to her, the heat from his body seeping instantaneously through the thin silk of her dress. "I did it...the real estate agent did it...what's the difference? The fact is you look beautiful in blue light. You look beautiful in any light."

She sensed the kiss before she felt it—his lips warm and sweet and tender. His mouth caressed hers softly, demanding nothing and promising everything. Both held tight to their wineglasses, not touching beyond the kiss, yet Harley's knees weakened. Grant countered her tiny wobble by bracing her with a hand on her arm.

He ended the kiss with a nibble. First on her lips, then across her cheek. Down her chin. Harley offered her throat and neck. He readily accepted, sampling her pulse points with delicate bites. Her skin purled like the surface of the Jacuzzi.

"So sweet. So soft."

She hardly noticed when he took away her wineglass, setting the full goblet beside his. He then clutched her hips firmly with both his hands and eased her forward. An inch of space remained between them, not quite near enough for touch, but more than adequate for his musky-scented body heat to make her dizzy.

In the turquoise glow, his eyes, two onyx stones, sparkled with iced fire. His cheekbones and chin, rugged and shadowed with stubble, seemed sharper. Edgier. More dangerous than a man like Grant had a right or the capacity to be. Yet Grant posed no risks to her well-being. Only her heart, and with it, her body and soul.

"I don't know if I like you in blue light." She traced down his cheek with her thumb, lightly indenting his shadowy skin. "You look almost…criminal."

"It's not the light." Husky and deep, his voice snared her, held her with the tenacity of a taut steel cord. "It's you. The thoughts you make me think are definitely illegal."

She flicked a fingernail over his lips, still wet and warm from their kiss. "Illegal, or just naughty?"

Pulling her close, he ground the rigid length of him against her belly. Instinctively, she rose on her tiptoes, pressing herself closer. Even the scanty barrier of her dress and lingerie seemed overwhelming. Extreme.

He smoothed his hands over her bare shoulders and down her arms. "Depends."

"On?"

He glanced at the gurgling hot tub. Steam wafted from the water, blanketing the tiled Jacuzzi with a misty haze. When his gaze returned to her, she witnessed the dusky smoldering of passion she'd come to crave. "Why don't we just start with naughty and see where we go from there?"

A tendril of air tickled her spine as he drew down the zipper on her dress.

"Aren't you afraid the neighbors might see?" she

asked, nearly losing her balance as he slid his hands up her back and unhooked her bra.

His chuckle matched the baritone rumblings from the spa. "I have twelve-foot hedges on either side of the yard and no neighbor in back. Unless old Willie Langley has binoculars that cut through solid brick, you're shielded from all prying eyes. Except mine."

He slipped the thin straps over her shoulders, then tugged until her dress and bra lay in a billowing blue mound at her feet. He stepped around her, perusing her from all angles, touching her here or there as it suited him, seducing her with an admiring stare.

She crossed her arms, somewhat intimidated by his scrutiny, but he immediately clucked his tongue and worked her protective stance loose.

"Don't get shy with me now, sweetheart. I'm just looking. Admiring." He traced a single finger across the small of her back. "Worshipping. I'd never get tired of looking at you. Never."

She hooked her fingers in the sides of her garter belt, wanting to put her hands somewhere, preferably on him, yet he remained about a foot away as he circled.

"I wouldn't mind something interesting to look at," she challenged, hoping he'd remove at least his shirt and tie so she wouldn't feel so vulnerable.

"All you had to do was ask."

One tug divested him of his bow tie. Ditto for the belt. Like a stalking cougar, he continued to circle her, popping one button, then another, until she could see the dark hair curling on his toned chest. Her breath abandoned her. Her breasts tingled. Her mouth sought a moisture only he could serve.

He unhooked his pants, leaving them lazily open on his hips as he had this afternoon. "I do believe I'm stripping for you. How'm I doing?"

"If you want my professional opinion, I don't remember."

"I don't care about your profession, Harley Roberts. I want your personal observations." He untucked his shirt and undid his cuff links. In a fluid motion, his shirt slid down his torso and then floated like a cloud as he tossed it onto a patio chair.

"I'd pay money to see you strip."

"Sorry, I don't take cash."

She turned with him, licking her lips as his pants dropped to the ground. "Credit cards? Checks?"

He shook his head, took her hands and led her to the water. "Nothing but trade, darling, nothing but trade."

11

HE STEPPED INTO the hot tub first, ditching his boxer shorts at the last moment and then submerging himself to his waist in the churning water. She moved to unsnap her nylons, but he stopped her. "Whoa, whoa. What's the rush?" He kissed her hands, licking the crevices between her fingers with a hot, moist tongue. "Let me find a better vantage point."

Easing away, he settled in one of the Jacuzzi's curved seats, his line of sight level with her knees. Looking up, he'd have an unhindered view of her every curve and crevice. "We don't have any veils," he commented, reminding her of his teasing at the wedding, "but this is good. Real good."

His flaming gaze amid the toasty steam heated Harley to the boiling point. Her breathing grew shallow. Her palms moistened. Grant waited, his eyes large with expectation, for her to peel away the last few bits of her clothing with all the finesse and bewitchery of an accomplished exotic dancer. She'd probably disrobed hundreds of times before, but never for such a special audience. She wanted to give Grant this fantasy more than anything—one she'd certainly given so many men before—men she didn't love.

Yet a chill lingered, just behind her, in the shadow of her past. She froze.

"Harley?"

Immediately, Grant recognized the cold shimmer of

anxiety glazing her eyes and keeping her still. He'd touched a raw spot—her stripping—reminding her of a part of her past she clearly didn't want to recall. He cursed himself for forgetting how truly tentative their relationship remained—and would remain until she recalled her former life.

Until then, he could only affect her present. Show her how much he cared. Sloshing across the tub, he took her quaking hand and flashed her what he hoped was his most seductive grin.

"On second thought, why don't you leave the stripping to the experts? Think the Chippendales would hire me?"

When the tiniest hint of a smile flexed her lips and she nodded, Grant kissed her palm and knelt on the step into the spa. Eye-level to her panties, he unhooked her garter belt, splaying one wet hand over the small of her back while the other held the lingerie tentatively in place.

"I suppose I should do this one leg at a time." He kissed her upper thigh, just below the garter, and traced the curve of her leg with his tongue. "But I'm not feeling patient. I don't think I can go that slowly." But he'd sure as hell try. He pressed his mouth against her panties, exhaling his hot breath, inhaling her feminine scent.

A soft groan and the combing of her fingers roughly through his hair urged him to release the garter belt and draw the hose down her smooth legs and over her wobbly feet. She continued to moan as he slid his hands beneath her panties and kneaded her firm buttocks. The fear, the hesitation he'd witnessed moments before, drifted away amidst the Jacuzzi steam.

With a stiff tongue, he stroked her, opened her, tasted her through the material, darkening the satiny blue with a mingling of his moisture and hers. Nipping, he caught flesh and silk between his teeth, intensifying her faint cries. She tugged his hair. Her head fell forward.

He snagged the edge of her underwear with his teeth and tugged them down and then off. She braced her hands on his shoulders, impaling him with her fingernails. He buried his face in the soft downy hair at the apex of her thighs, laving her gently while he lifted her into the water.

In slow inches, he loosened his grip, sliding her down his body while he kissed the line from mons to navel to cleavage. She wrapped her arms around his neck and her legs around his waist, stopping her descent when they were nearly sex to sex, her nipples dark and pouting and pointed at his mouth.

She groaned when he bit her, cooed when he suckled, cried out when he flicked her pebbled nipples in rapid succession. She squirmed until her sweet folds captured the tip of his erection, urging him to enter her body here and now.

"Oh, Grant. I want you inside me."

Growling, he cupped her buttocks and lifted her higher, breaking their tentative connection. He unwrapped her legs and lowered her thigh high into the water. "Not just yet, sweetheart."

He kissed her until he knew she wouldn't protest, then reached over the side of the Jacuzzi to his pants. He took two packaged condoms from his pocket, tore one from the other, threw the first on the edge of the hot tub and tossed the second into the adjacent pool.

Her eyes lit with mischievous curiosity.

"Are we going diving for condoms?"

He pushed her back gently until she fell into the curved seat. Bending over her, he captured her lips and thrust his tongue against hers, tasting the sweet mingling of wine and steam while he eased her legs apart. "Soon. But first, I have some more dangerous diving to do. For a particular pearl."

Grant eased down until only his face remained above the waves. Water rumbled in his ears. Harley shifted in the popping bubbles and hazy steam, her breasts alternately slipping from sight, her arms outstretched on the tiled ledge, her eyes half open and locked with his.

Once she settled in, he joined the churning water in kissing her parted thighs, savoring the combined flavors of chlorine and honeyed flesh. He buoyed his hands beneath her buttocks, lifting her high. With the pumping jets pounding him from all sides and his lungs holding tight to his breath, he took her sweet center in his mouth. The sultry water made her warm and pliant. He eased her knees over his shoulders. She stiffened, then squirmed.

He came up for a quick breath, then dove into her again. His heartbeat pounded in his ears, even over the growling of the jets. When her bud hardened between his teeth and tongue, he knew she had reached the edge. The sound of her pleasured cries lured him to the surface.

He gasped when he rose, but Harley allowed him no time to breathe. Her lips boldly captured his. Her hands clasped his cheeks and held him immobile. She fed him air and love and passion—all in a single unyielding kiss. This was the woman he'd almost lost when those low-life creeps abducted her, and then again when he'd suggested she strip for him.

But now, the bold, fearless woman he'd grown to adore returned.

He slipped his mouth away from hers in a desperate

rush to ease the torching of his deprived lungs. Gasping, he touched her as the water touched her, furiously and haphazardly, and with ever-escalating heat. She suckled his neck and shoulders, panting between bites, stroking his sex with her hands. Desire raged through him like a flash flood.

He was hard. Rock hard. Harder than he'd ever, ever been. If he drove into her now, he'd surely break her in two. His body, so close to shutting out his voice of reason, demanded immediate release.

With his last tentative grasp on sanity, he scooped Harley into his arms, took the single step to the ledge, then plunged them both into the icy water of the swimming pool.

When they broke the surface, Harley screamed. "It's freezing!"

Grant continued to hold her as she splashed and spluttered, enjoying the feel of her prickly gooseflesh and stony nipples against his chest. His muscles shuddered and protested at the instantaneous change in temperature, but the thought of rekindling her heat kept him hard and ready. "Mmm. I'll warm you, honey."

Her smile grew dark and daring as she calmed and ran her fingers through his dripping hair. "You've done quite enough. When is it my turn?"

"When I'm finished with you."

"And that will be?"

Never, he hoped, but he bit back the reply. She wasn't any more prepared for a commitment than he, especially not one destined to end badly. If Howell Phipps, the town gossips, her cousin Moana, that scum-bucket Buck and Harley's memory loss unwittingly combined forces, Harley and he didn't stand a chance. For the present, they could share only what they had now—intense passion—with mutual caring and respect on the side.

"I'll be finished when I make you as crazy as you make me."

He released his hold on her and dove deep beneath the surface, his eyes honed on the red, square package dotting the bottom of the pool. Snagging the condom, he propelled to the surface with a powerful thrust, grabbing Harley along the way. He locked her legs around his waist then half swam, half kicked them to the shallow end.

Settling on the middle step, he positioned her atop him. In defiance of his quest for control, she shimmied until her feminine lips enveloped his shaft, cloaking him in warmth, yet denying him entrance.

She kissed the sluicing water from his face and ran her hands down his torso. "I am crazy. Crazy for you."

He buried his face between her breasts. "Trust me, honey, you don't know crazy like I do."

With a limber tongue, he lapped at the droplets clinging to her skin, swirling thick circles around her areolas, avoiding her rigid nipples to enhance her burning need. She exhaled rhythmic gasps that sometimes sounded like his name, urging him to pleasure her deeper, to return her to the orgasmic rush he'd brought her to before.

Her hips undulated, easing him closer inside her. With a groan, he stretched out of reach. If he remained pressed against her, he'd come before she did. He throbbed for release so acutely, his blood pounded in his ears. His eyes couldn't focus. He lost the power of speech. She whimpered, but acquiesced when he filled the empty space with his hand. One finger, then two, probed her hidden recesses, taunting her with reserved half thrusts.

But he wasn't ready for climax. Not yet. Not until he taught her how no other man, no other lover could ever satisfy her completely—heart, body and soul—as he did. Once certain of that, how could she ever leave him?

Yet Harley had no such agenda. With her toes, she tickled his thick sacs, then drew her foot up and down, stroking him beneath the water. He took her nipple then, punishing her with his teeth.

Her cry embodied the sweetest rapture he'd ever heard. She grabbed his cheeks and held him to her breast, kissing his forehead and whispering a jumble of words, some unintelligible, others that fired his soul. He suckled her thoroughly, until a slickness met his fingers where he caressed her.

He could wait no longer.

He flipped over and dragged his pulsing body to the uppermost step, leaving only his rear end in the water. Before he could tear open the red packet, Harley's mouth encircled him, teasing and plying and sucking. He nearly dropped the condom back into the pool's cool depths, but she stole the latex from his grasp, sheathed him and sat atop him, sliding his sex inside with a feminine, yet guttural gasp.

The tile bit into his back, but Grant didn't care. The warm night air swirled in bursts—breezy, then gusty, mirroring the thrusts he pumped into her white-hot center. She sat up straight, slicked back her wet hair and arched her back with feline elegance.

He heard himself uttering words resembling a sacred litany, but couldn't form a coherent thought. He clutched Harley's buttocks, bolstering and guiding her deliberate rhythm. When she scooped handfuls of water to trickle over her pointed nipples, the first wave of molten fire drained from him to her.

A blur of motion followed. Raw. Demanding. He took her breast in his mouth, slid his hand between them, inciting her instantaneous climax. She screamed. His accompanying explosion echoed like deep bass to her piercing aria. He crashed into her with a ferocity she not only matched, but exceeded. With his final thrust, he lifted them off the step and splashed their joined bodies into the dark blue water.

HARLEY KNEW NOW what drowning felt like. Not the terror or the agony, but the helplessness. Locked to Grant, she merely held on while he spun them beneath the surface, bringing them up for breath then plunging them under the water in an undulating ritual that cleansed her like a pagan baptism.

He finally pulled her out of the water near the steps to the Jacuzzi, settling her on the cradle of his lap, his touch tentative, his kisses soft. A few minutes passed before she'd gathered enough air in her lungs to speak.

"Was that crazy enough for you?" she asked.

Nuzzling her neck, he hummed his denial against her skin. "It's a start. We have all night to find true insanity."

"Is once ever enough for you?"

"Is it for you?"

She pulled herself out of his arms to the pool deck, her muscles weak and shaky, but pleasantly so. Smiling wickedly, she eluded his grasp and sauntered to the table, watching him watch her. She swiveled her naked hips just a bit more than she would normally, enjoying the play of refreshed need on his features. She retrieved her wineglass and relieved her cottony mouth with a generous swallow. The sweet blush slid like ice down her parched throat, yet his gaze, even from a few feet away, sent a heated torrent spiraling through her.

She refilled both glasses and returned to the Jacuzzi. "I didn't thank you for rescuing me."

He lifted himself to the edge, swung his feet into the Jacuzzi, took his glass then guided her to sit beside him.

"Those people didn't want to hurt you, or they would have."

She took another sip of wine, hoping the alcohol would dispel a sudden chill. "But they want to hurt Buck. And maybe Moana. If she is my cousin, I can't let that happen."

"We won't let that happen. I'll call Mac in the morning. We'll work something out." He turned his goblet between both hands, his eyes cast down, his lips pursed, as if he contemplated some great irony in the rose-tinted liquid. "It wasn't a very exciting rescue. If I were Mac, I'd have rushed in, guns and badge blazing."

Harley covered her amusement with another sip of wine. She wasn't accustomed to Grant acting so boyish, so unsure of himself, so…normal. And yet, she had to clear up his misconception without delay. She may have just met Mac's wife, but the memory of Jenna's sad eyes boiled her blood. "If you were Mac, you would have spent the evening ignoring me."

Grant shrugged then swallowed a quarter of his glass. "Mac loves Jenna. He's just a little…obsessed. With his job. With what other people think about the way he does his job. He'll come to his senses."

Harley didn't answer. Who was she to judge someone else's relationship when theirs was based on fantasy and half-known truths? At least Mac and Jenna had time to fix whatever was so obviously wrong with their marriage. She and Grant wouldn't have that luxury.

Grant put his arm around her waist and pulled her closer. Coupled with the slightly rough tile grazing her bare backside, his touch reminded her that only moments would pass before she'd need him inside her again. Before she surrendered, a few things needed saying.

She took another sip to steel herself for her confession. "I overheard Mr. Phipps talking to you at the wedding. After we danced."

His shoulders stiffened, but he continued to sip his wine as if her revelation meant nothing. "Don't mind him. He'd had too much champagne."

She pressed her forehead against his shoulder, breathing in his scent, a mixed aroma of sex and chlorine and musk. "That's not true and you know it."

After draining his glass, he climbed back into the hot tub, easing her down with him. "You want me to tell you what's true, Harley? Howell Phipps can't run the firm without me. He lost his instinct for the market years ago. Up until a few days ago, I'd forgotten that fact. Let him make his threats. When push comes to shove, he can't touch me."

"He could replace you."

Grant wrapped his arms around her and pulled her full to him, hard and ready again. "He won't."

"You don't really know that. If he finds something really horrible in my past, he could destroy your reputation."

He kissed the top of her head. "Stop worrying about me. I'm more concerned about what he'd do to you."

She believed him, though she couldn't muster any real fear of Howell Phipps. Not for herself anyway. Grant's capacity to place her needs above his embodied the main reason she loved him so deeply. And why she didn't dare stay in his house past tomorrow morning.

"I don't belong in his world...or yours. In my world, whatever that man says or does won't mean a thing."

Grant growled low and took her cheeks between his palms, tilting her head so her gaze met his, blue irises to brown. "Harley Roberts, you are my world."

Her breath caught in her throat and a band of iron seemed to wrap around her heart, squeezing until she gasped. Grant didn't know what he was saying. The sensational sex had clouded his usually razor-sharp brain. "Please, Grant. You know that can't be true."

"Why can't it? Because you haven't regained your full memory? Because you might be a stripper? Because your cousin might have a criminal connection?"

Harley knew she'd never find the will to leave tomorrow if he continued down this road. He was wrong. Dead wrong. She accepted responsibility for his delusional thinking. She'd led him into a series of fantasies where anything and everything was possible—where two people from different dimensions of the universe connected and thrived.

Yet tonight, she'd learned just how reality would squash those dreams like a meaty fist on an ant. Despite his reassurances, she'd heard the power in Howell Phipps's threats. The venom in his tone. But mostly, she recalled how Grant had had to rescue her. How she'd had to cling to him to find relief from her fear. Grant's caring bolstered her like a crutch. Without doubt, she'd never cajole her mind into recovering her lost memories so long as she had Grant to keep her pain at bay.

"I don't want to talk anymore." She kissed his chin

and smoothed her naked breasts against the soft hair on his chest. "I want to know more about insanity."

His groan was resigned, but his smile ignited a thrill that burned all rational thought from her head. "Then just look to me, sweetheart. These last few days with you, I've become an expert."

HARLEY DECIDED GRANT'S parents must never have let him sleep late. Despite his desire for her to join him at his grandmother's for breakfast, he'd accepted her sleepy "maybe later" without a smidgen of argument. He'd simply kissed her nose, drawn the sheet over her and promised to call her at noon.

She jumped when the phone rang at nine-thirty, only twenty minutes after she'd heard Grant's sport utility vehicle roll over the driveway and she'd begun to dress. She almost didn't answer, afraid he'd phoned her from the car. Not wanting to alert him to her plan to leave long before his twelve o'clock call, she picked up the receiver.

"Hello?"

Silence answered, though Harley thought she heard the rumble of traffic in the background.

She tried again. "Hello?"

This time, she heard a distinctly feminine, though shaky voice. "Hailey?"

"Excuse me? Who are you calling for?"

"God, please let this be the number. I'm looking for my cousin, Hailey Roberts. I got this number from my friend, Joy. She said some rich guy gave it to her, and that I could find..."

"Moana?"

"Hailey? Lord, girl, you never call me by my stage name. Is something wrong?"

Hailey? Stage name? Harley bent her knees slowly,

letting the mattress catch her before she fell into a swirling dizziness.

"A lot is wrong. More than I should discuss over the phone. Where are you? There are people after you, do you know that? You shouldn't go back to your condo."

Moana's snort overrode the background noise. "I already made that mistake, but I booked before anyone saw me. I'm at a rest stop outside of Plant City. Joy said you were staying in Citrus Hill. Isn't that where that guy from the bachelor party lived? Is it him? I mean, I knew you could pull off the gig, but I didn't think you'd move in."

"I haven't. Well, I have, but only temporarily. Until I found you. Can you meet me?"

"Give me the address. I'll ask for directions when I hit the exit."

Harley bit her bottom lip, reluctant to bring more scandal on Grant if someone discovered not one, but two strippers holed up in his house.

"No, that wouldn't be a good idea. I know which rest stop you're at—I saw it on my way to Tampa. Hang tight. I'll meet you there in thirty minutes, okay?"

The hesitation in Moana's voice clutched Harley's lungs. This woman was Harley's only link to her past, and to the boy whose sweet face haunted her dreams.

"Yeah, sure. But don't piss around, okay? After the wreck those punks did to my place, I don't think I should stay in one place too long."

Harley agreed to hurry and gently hung up the phone. Without allowing time for regrets or what-ifs, she threw her measly collection of clothes and makeup into a tote bag she found in Grant's closet and headed downstairs. She didn't have much choice but to take Grant's Mercedes, rationalizing that she'd find a way to return the car soon after reuniting with Moana. Telling herself she had no time for notes, she grabbed Gus's phone number and Grant's extra set of car keys from his study and left.

The drive to the Plant City rest area took fifteen minutes—just long enough for Harley to realize how impossible leaving Grant forever would be. Emotional crutch or not, the man had seared himself into her soul. She loved him. Respected him. Needed him. Maybe once she'd regained her memory and fell back into the regular patterns of her life, she'd manage to see the last few days for the innocuous diversion they were.

Or maybe she'd find a way back into his life.

When she caught sight of Moana leaning against the rusted door of a Chevy Impala probably older than she was, Harley thought twice.

She pulled the Mercedes alongside and studied the woman's face, positive her features matched those of the young girl in the photo she'd shoved in her tote bag. When Harley rolled down the Mercedes' tinted glass window, Moana's smile of recognition matched the grin in the picture—full over the lips and teeth, but just failing to reach the eyes. Apparently, happiness didn't come easily to women in her family.

Moana whistled long and appreciatively, running her hand lightly over the shiny black paint job. "Buck would freak if he saw you behind the wheel of this. Where's your banker?"

Harley bristled at the sound of Buck's name, but shook her fear away and stepped out of the car. "Grant doesn't know I'm here."

Moana hissed out a curse. "Now you're a car thief? This is big trouble you don't know about."

"Trouble and me have become well acquainted in the past few days."

Harley noticed then that Moana kept her gaze focused on the entrance to the rest area, only glancing her way when she spoke. A half-dozen cigarette butts lay flattened by Moana's feet. Her fingernails, still sporting spots of bright vermilion coating, had been chewed to the quick.

With her hand as a sun shield, Harley joined Moana in scoping out the line of semitrucks and recreational vehicles parked on the other side of the rest area, across from a pavilion with public washrooms and vending machines. After a few seconds, she realized she had no idea for whom she searched. "Were you followed?"

Moana shook her head, but with her bottom lip clutched between her teeth, she didn't look one hundred percent certain.

"I've been on the run for two days straight, then I get back to the condo and find it trashed. By the time I reached Joy, I was pretty freaked. She told me Riva was looking for me. For me! They think I can lead them to Buck."

"Can't you?"

Moana leaned her jean-clad hips on the side panel of her rusted car and slid a cigarette from the pocket of her vest, a sweet daisy print worn in contrast over a tight, ribbed tank top. "I left that jerk in Valdosta the minute I realized his guys did your carjacking."

"Carjacking?"

Moana tore a match from a wilted book and lit her cigarette. "Damn. Joy wasn't kidding, was she?" Moana cupped her hand beneath Harley's chin and gazed deep into her eyes. "You don't remember me."

Harley leaned back on the door of the Mercedes and shook her head. "I can't remember anything before Thursday night."

"Then how did you know who I was when you drove up?"

Harley reached into the car and pulled out the acrylic frame. She handed the photo to Moana, suddenly wishing she smoked so she'd have something to do with her hands other than fidget or thrust them into her pockets.

Moana chuckled at the picture. "I noticed this was missing from my place. Thought Riva'd snatched it to show around, since it's the only picture I had with me in it. It's old, but I guess we kind of look the same. 'Cept for Sammy."

Harley took the photo back when Moana offered it. She traced the chubby face of the chocolate-covered toddler. "Sammy. He's my…"

She looked up at Moana, her inflection posing the question.

"Your baby brother. Your parents died when he was only one. You were twelve. You came to live with me and Momma. Life went downhill from there."

Nodding, Harley clutched the photo tight to her chest as she'd done the night before while hiding from Riva and her henchmen. Her heart ached to find Sammy, but the pain diminished now that she knew she could.

"You can't even remember Sammy? Have you seen a doctor?"

"No, but I will. As soon as I find out where I live."

Moana took a long drag of her cigarette, then blew the smoke away from them. "Girl, as of today, you and me are homeless. You left Momma's about a week ago. You swore not to go back, except to get Sammy when you had a place."

A week ago? That didn't make sense. Yet it did. Now she knew why Joy and the others from the local strip clubs didn't know who she was. She was a stranger to the area.

"You had a studio hooked up, but then one of Buck's gang jacked your car and your cash. You came to stay with me at the condo. And we can't go back there."

"A studio? For what?"

Shaking her head, Moana watched as another line of cars pulled off the interstate into the rest area. "You're a physical therapist. You use dance to help people recover from accidents or diseases."

"I'm not a stripper?"

Even the air horn from a nearby semi couldn't cover Moana's raucous laughter. "A stripper? Honey, this job for the banker would have been your first and your last. You did it because you needed the cash or you'd lose your studio. Which you probably have." Moana flicked a line of ash to the ground.

Harley's legs nearly buckled. "A therapist? But the costumes? I remembered a closet full of really skimpy costumes."

Moana shook her head. "Momma had you ballroom dancing from the minute you showed a lick of talent. You won a ton of championships, made a good load of cash and scholarships. Unfortunately, you let Momma talk you into a joint account. What Buck's creeps stole was all you had left." She dropped her cigarette, pressed it flat beneath her boot and gazed at Harley through squinting eyes. "You really don't remember me?"

Her mind swimming with the new information, Harley concentrated hard in order to answer. "I'm sorry. I don't even know what your real name is."

Moana chuckled and coughed at the same time. "Baby, half the time, I don't remember that either.

You've been the only one to call me Mary Jo in a long, long time."

Mary Jo. Hailey. So close to their "stage" names and yet worlds apart. Mary Jo and Hailey matched the girls in the faded photograph, but not the women they were now. The names oozed innocence. Simplicity.

Suddenly, Moana muttered a venomous string of curses that caused Harley's nerves to stand on end and shiver.

"I know that truck. Damn, damn, damn." Grabbing her purse from the Impala, Moana ran around to the passenger side of the Mercedes and popped open the door. Her skin paled. Her eyes widened in fear. "Don't just stand there! Get us the hell out of here."

12

GRANT PULLED PAST the tall brick gates of Wellesley Manor with only one thing on his mind—buying Harley a beeper. For the second time in just under four days, his phone calls to her went unanswered. He'd called three times since arriving at his grandmother's house, but only reached his answering machine. When concern turned to worry, then to anger and back to worry, he decided to return home. She had been hit on the head a few days ago, he rationalized. She'd been kidnapped the night before. Who knew if she needed him, or if she was just basking poolside and couldn't hear the phone?

Gus encouraged Grant to leave, not bothering to cover an omniscient smile. His grandmother, only half-informed regarding who Harley was and why she was staying at Grant's house, merely patted his arm and told him to follow his heart.

For once, Grant would. His entire life, he'd chosen the path dictated by his logic or by his sense of responsibility. In the eighteen years of his adulthood, he rarely let his emotions rule his actions. Except for the one time he'd tried to save his marriage. He'd failed, mostly because listening to his heart instead of his brain would have kept him from marrying Camille in the first place.

He wouldn't make the same mistakes with Harley. They'd made love several times last night. In the pool.

The hot tub. The pool deck. The stairs. His bed. Not once had he admitted how deep his feelings went for her—how completely he loved her—how he couldn't imagine living another minute without her permanently in his life. He'd already asked Gus for the name and number of a specialist to help her overcome her amnesia, and he didn't care who found out. She could never completely accept love and commitment from him until she remembered her past. If he lost his job for being in love, so be it.

He turned onto his street, invigorated by his choice, fortified by his unbound love. He hardly noticed the bright blue pickup parked askew on his curb and driveway until he spotted his Mercedes blocked behind it.

Then he saw Harley standing on the lawn, her right arm extended to protect a screaming redhead standing behind her. Harley swung her left arm fruitlessly at a thin man stalking them head-on. Grant threw his vehicle into park without hitting the brake, jerking himself forward and causing his seat belt to nearly choke him.

Harley kicked the man, connecting with his kneecap, but not slowing his attack.

"Buck! Don't hurt her," shouted the redhead, whom Grant guessed was Harley's cousin, Moana. "She's got nothing to do with us!"

Buck grabbed Harley by the neck and yanked her forward, ignoring Moana's plea. Mercilessly, Buck slapped Harley with the back of his hand, tossed her aside and clutched Moana around the neck.

"Harley!" In seconds, Grant released his seat belt and maneuvered around the cars and through his security gate. He attacked without pause, striking Buck full force in the neck joint.

Harley remained motionless on the grass. Moana screamed. Buck cursed, releasing Moana as he went sprawling onto Grant's manicured lawn.

Buck charged like an enraged bull, his head aimed at Grant's midsection. Shifting, Grant shot a left hook to Buck's jaw. Still standing, Buck roared, his black eyes slants of rage. Blood oozed from the corner of his mouth.

"This ain't your fight, rich boy. I just want what's mine, then I'm gone."

Moana, who'd slid to the ground beside Harley, met Buck's stare with equal fury. "I ain't yours no more. You're nothing but a low-life thief! And a dead one, too. That guy in Miami's gonna slice your throat. And I'm gonna ask if I can watch."

Buck lunged toward Moana, who screamed and covered Harley with her body. Grant kicked Buck in the gut, sending him spinning like a top until he landed on the grass with a thud.

Sirens wailed in the background. Grant glanced quickly over his shoulder, catching sight of Wilhelmina Langley shooting from her front door, her portable phone clutched to her ear.

When Buck started crawling back toward the women, Grant stopped him by pressing his foot to the back of his neck. Buck growled as Grant increased the pressure.

Grant suddenly gained a strong affection for his steel-toed work boots. "Looks like you made it my fight. Spread your arms out so I can see them."

A swarm of Citrus Hill police officers spilled onto the lawn, guns drawn and shouting orders. Only when a uniformed policewoman pressed the barrel of her gun to the back of Buck's neck did Grant retreat.

Moana helped her cousin sit up. Harley's enlarged

pupils turned her blue eyes a frightening shade of black. A dark red mark shadowed the entire left side of her face. Grant knelt in front of her and took her hands, not certain which of them shook more violently.

"Harley. Are you all right? Say something, honey."

She blinked. Once. Twice. The quick flutter of lashes seemed to finally clear the stupor from her eyes.

"Grant?" She turned to the woman beside her. "Mary Jo?" She let go of one of Grant's hands and grasped the redhead at the elbow. "Mary Jo! I remember. Good Lord—" her eyes, now glossy and beaming, sought Grant "—I remember!"

The cops, directed by Mrs. Langley, descended on the trio like a ravenous horde. One policeman radioed for the ETA on the ambulance, another verified the location as the First Financial corporate mansion. Another officer pushed Grant aside, insisting Harley remain still until the paramedics arrived.

Grant opened his mouth to argue when a rookie officer approached, his youthful eyes darting from Grant's clenched fists to Buck, who still lay handcuffed on the grass. "We need a statement to make the arrest and get this creep off your lawn, Mr. Riordan."

Harley's eyes, at first wondrously round, suddenly clouded, as if something terrible—perhaps that traumatic event Gus warned of—flashed into her mind.

A few feet away, Moana—no, Mary Jo—Harley's cousin, judging by her resemblance to the teenager in the photograph Harley had taken from the condominium, relayed her version of the incident to a policewoman. She seemed to be providing all the facts they needed to remand the cretin straight to the local jailhouse.

"Not now," Grant warned.

The cop lightly placed his hand on Grant's shoulder.

"It'll just take a few minutes. Mrs. Langley will take care of the young woman, won't you, ma'am?"

His nemesis already had Harley on her feet and her arm around her shoulder. With a careless wave, she bypassed the officer who insisted they wait for the ambulance. Mrs. Langley appeared genuinely concerned and, Grant had to admit, she did have law enforcement falling into step.

"Go on, son. She just needs a minute or two to settle down. And that man's presence," Mrs. Langley said as she indicated Buck with a disdainful tilt of her head, "won't help matters."

Harley's gaze locked on Buck. A dark horror spread over her face, pursing her lips and squinting her eyes. Grant wasn't sure if Harley was about to attack the man or run screaming in the opposite direction, but he wouldn't wait to find out. He nodded his agreement to Mrs. Langley, who led Harley away.

"Three minutes. That's the limit." Grant followed the officer to his cruiser. The sooner he got that jerk off his lawn, the sooner he could rescue Harley from Mrs. Langley's dubious good intentions.

Three minutes turned into fifteen as the officer embellished their interview with information about Buck's criminal past. Law enforcement officials all over South Central Florida knew and had been looking for Mary Jo's boyfriend—including Mac's team at the Tampa Police Department. As the officer completed the report, Grant put in a quick call to Mac from his cell phone, then waited impatiently to sign the complaint.

"We'll contact you if we need anything else, Mr. Riordan, but I doubt we will. This guy dug a deep grave even before he attacked Ms. Roberts and her cousin." The officer handed Grant a copy of the report and returned his driver's license. "He's a dangerous character. It's a good thing you came along."

Yeah, he was a real hero. He may have saved Harley once again from physical harm, but he'd abandoned her to the control and influence of Wilhelmina Langley for the past twenty minutes. With the news story of the year playing out just across the street from her, Langley had to be foaming at the mouth.

Grant walked past the open driveway gate as a dark sedan with the license plate "PHIPP-1" maneuvered around the three police cars, ambulance and fire truck blocking most of Wellesley Lane. Moments later, Howell Phipps emerged from the sedan wearing pastel-colored golf duds and the most horrified expression Grant had seen since the market dropped over two hundred points in a single hour.

"What the hell is going on here?" the old man barked.

Grant pulled in a deep breath and released the air with deliberate slowness. He wondered if today was Friday the thirteenth. Maybe April Fool's Day. He couldn't imagine the situation getting worse.

"Nothing you need to be concerned with, Mr. Phipps. The fun's over and everything is under control." *Except me.* "Why don't you return to the country club? We'll discuss this in the morning."

Grant started up the drive when Phipps, surprisingly spry for a man his age, caught up to him. "Now, see here, Riordan. The police chief summoned me off the course with the report of a disturbance at my CEO's home. A home my company owns, I should remind you."

"You don't need to remind me. Every slick surface and piece of sterile furniture reminds me."

His boss halted, his eyes round and red with rage.

"My wife decorated that house herself. How dare you insult her. What's gotten into you lately?"

Grant slung his hands into his pockets and faced his employer, not entirely contrite. Suddenly, Grant hated every square foot of the grand house behind them, mostly because the structure mirrored him so accurately—pretentious, impersonal, soulless—at least, until Harley had stepped through the doorway. "I didn't intend any disrespect to your wife. But I really don't have the time or the inclination to deal with you right now. Two women were just attacked on my front lawn. I'd like to go make sure they are both all right."

Phipps's cheeks puffed, making him look like an outraged blowfish. "Deal with me? You seem to have forgotten quite a bit in your tangle with that miscreant. I am your superior."

Grant continued toward the house as he spoke. "You are my employer, Mr. Phipps, not my superior. And under the circumstances, you'll have to settle for my undivided attention during work hours."

Phipps stopped Grant's forward motion by clamping him firmly on the shoulder. With adrenaline still surging through his veins, Grant's will alone kept him from meeting Phipps's interference with the same rage he'd unleashed on Buck.

"What's gotten into you, Grant? That woman is nothing to you. My sources haven't positively identified her, but I know she's no relation. And this incident illustrates her unsuitability. This fiasco will make grand fodder for Langley's column. Thankfully, it's Sunday and this week's edition is already delivered. We have an entire week to exert some damage control before the next issue."

Grant chose to ignore Phipps's "nothing to you" assessment. This wasn't the time to open a dialogue on his personal life. In fact, there had never been a time. Disgust filled him as he realized how much of his pride he'd swallowed in the name of professionalism and success. How much he'd nearly sacrificed in his attempt to hide the magnitude of Harley's presence in his life—both from his boss and from himself.

Well, not anymore.

"You do that, Mr. Phipps. Exert away."

"Of course, that won't take care of the local editions of the *Tampa Tribune* or *Orlando Sentinel*. This is, after all, a criminal matter now. Perhaps if I speak to the police chief..."

While Phipps mused, Grant stalked away. He couldn't care less if the fight on his lawn made front-page headlines, as long as Harley wasn't hurt. She'd said something about regaining her memory before the police officer dragged him away. Just how much did she remember? Enough to at last feel confident about their relationship? Or would the truth about her past end the glorious four days he'd discovered in her company?

Harley sat alone on the front steps, her knees drawn up to her chest, cradling her forehead. Something about her position alerted him to exercise caution. He balanced one foot on the bottom step and clutched the inner lining of his pockets to fight his impulse to touch her.

"Harley? Honey, are you okay?"

She rocked her head on her knees, her face hidden beneath a curtain of tangled hair. "I'm not sure."

He bit the inside of his cheek. "Are you hurt?"

When she looked up, her eyes, determined and stoic, glistened with moisture. "I'll be okay. I may have a shiner by morning, but..."

"That's my fault. I shouldn't have left you alone."

"It's not your fault." She slapped her thighs for emphasis. "None of this is. If you only knew who I was, what I've been through, you wouldn't say that. You'd know not to ever, ever say that!"

The time for caution elapsed. A single teardrop slipped down her cheek, still mottled red from Buck's handprint. Unwanted and unbidden, he pulled her into his arms.

She struggled against him, beating his chest. "No. You can't fix this for me!"

"I don't want to fix it," Grant lied. "I just want to help. Tell me what you remembered."

He loosened his grasp. She calmed. After a moment, she slipped from his embrace and resumed her seat on the brick steps. She toyed with her shoelaces, taking deep, cleansing breaths. Mrs. Langley emerged from a side door with a glass of water in one hand and the iced gel pack in the other. After catching sight of Grant, she placed both items on an outer windowsill and silently retreated into the house, closing the door behind her.

"My parents died when I was twelve." Harley's admission arrested Grant's attention from Mrs. Langley's oddly compassionate behavior. "My brother, Sammy, and I went to live with my Aunt Gracie in Miami."

Grant hesitated, then decided to sit beside her. He allowed a safe distance between them, leaning his elbows on his knees and lacing his fingers together to keep from reaching out to her while his touch remained unwelcome. "Sammy's the child in the photo?"

A tiny smile curved her lips, reassuring Grant of her strength. "He's sixteen now. A real computer whiz." The grin disappeared, leaving Grant to wonder if he'd seen it at all. "Anyway, Gracie wasn't too thrilled to have two more mouths to feed. She was raising Mary Jo alone as it was."

"But she kept you with her."

Harley smoothed her hands on her shorts, as if she itched to touch him, but fought the impulse. "She liked playing the martyr, vying for everyone's sympathy. Mary Jo wasn't a cooperative child and I was eager to please, to make sure Sammy and I didn't go to foster care or get separated. When she found out I could dance, she decided to turn my talent to her advantage."

Harley briefly recounted her childhood of daily dance classes, weekend recitals and grueling contests. When she turned fourteen, Grace set her sights on ballroom dancing, where the atmosphere proved classy and winning competitions became financially lucrative. When Harley turned fifteen, Gracie had paired Harley with a dancer named Paul, the eighteen-year-old boy who would later become her fiancé.

"He bailed for a job in New York just before the biggest contest of our career. The prize was a ten-thousand-dollar scholarship. I was already in graduate school and I needed the money to finish my internship, which was the only way for me to earn my certification as a dance therapist. But Paul didn't care about that, or our engagement. He conveniently forgot how I helped him land that job in New York—the agent who placed him saw us dance on television. I found out later the agent was interested in me too, but Paul convinced him I wouldn't be willing to relocate."

"Would you have?"

Harley paused, then shook her head. "No, but that wasn't the point. He knew firsthand how manipulative Grace was—and how badly I wanted to get Sammy away from her. He promised to take care of us, and I loved him for that. Then he betrayed me. He almost wrecked my future. And I almost let him."

"But you didn't."

Harley waved his comment away. "I decided then and there that I wouldn't let myself rely on anyone else ever again. I found another dance partner and won that contest. And several others. I finished school and signed a contract for a studio in Tampa, away from Gracie and her manipulations. I even contacted hospitals and clinics that were interested in dance therapy for their patients. I had everything under control. Planned out. Then Grace drained our joint checking account in a snit over my newfound independence."

"She stole from you?"

"She said I owed her for all the years she'd clothed and fed us. Paid for my dance lessons and Sammy's computer equipment." The lines around Harley's eyes hardened at the memory. "But my parents didn't leave us destitute. Their life insurance policy paid for nearly all of our expenses. Except the dancing, which was Grace's idea anyway. And Sammy's an industrious kid. He's mowed lawns and washed cars to pay for whatever computer gadgets he's wanted. But no matter what we did, we were always a burden. Trouble. That's why I can't let him stay with her."

Grant shook his head. He inched his hand nearer to her, hoping she'd accept the gesture. "She took so much from you. Not just money."

Harley folded her arms across her chest. "But she didn't get everything. She forgot the fifteen-hundred-dollar CD I'd won a few years before. I cashed it in and planned to use five hundred for the first month's rent on the studio and the remaining thousand on furniture, equipment and expenses until business picked up. I figured I could send for Sammy as soon as school let out for the summer. We'd be on our own. We might struggle, but we'd be happy."

Harley exhaled as her eyes drifted closed. Despite the defeated expression weighing her features, Grant saw only the clever, inventive woman he'd fallen head-over-heels in love with. She faced adversity with the same passion and fire she'd exhibited on the dance floor—and when making love to him. The same passion and fire he coveted, even emulated, solely because of her influence.

Yet she found little comfort in her accomplishments and even less pride in her past. Whatever traumatic incident triggered her amnesia seemed to obstruct her confidence like a thick stone wall.

"We don't have to talk about this now, Harley. Why don't we just go inside, pour some wine…"

"Grant, please." Her voice brimmed with barely checked irritation. "I don't want wine. I don't want to calm down. I want to tell you this so you'll understand. So I'll understand."

Grant's chest constricted. He didn't want to understand. Understanding meant accepting the distance Harley had already placed between them. He'd heard more than enough already to know where this tale would lead.

Yet she took his silence for agreement and continued. "I hated leaving Sammy, but I planned to send for him as soon as he'd finished the school year and I had a decent place for us to live. On my way to the studio to pay the last part of my deposit, I decided to visit Mary Jo. She'd run away from Grace years before, but we'd always kept in touch. I went to the club where she worked, but she wasn't there. I headed to her apartment. Not ten minutes later—" Harley rammed her fingers through her hair, then clung to the ends with brutal tension. "—I was carjacked. At gunpoint. About half a block from her place. They took everything."

Grant swallowed hard, pressing down the multitude of soothing words he wanted to croon to her, and the angry words he wanted to spit at no one in particular. In a red haze, he pictured a gun barrel shoved in Harley's face. He imagined her terror. Her vulnerability. Her life could have been snuffed out by a street thug's bullet—her body left in the street. He'd heard stories about carjackers who murdered their victims without a second thought—even those who cooperated.

"That was probably what you didn't want to remember."

She shook her head. "Only partly. The last straw was coming here. I needed quick cash. The landlord had another offer on my studio and I needed the five hundred to keep him to our deal. Mary Jo offered Steve's bachelor party. Taking off my clothes for money horrified me, but I was desperate. I had to send for Sammy. Save my career. It was one night. I could do it." Tenacity clung to her words as if she meant to convince herself all over again. Suddenly, her tone changed to a small whisper. "Then I saw you."

"Me?"

A smile fluttered across her lips, then disappeared like a naughty sprite. "You were on the phone on the patio. I caught one glimpse of you and knew I couldn't go through with the act. You were too powerful, too magnetic. In control. Just the type of man a woman like me should give a wide, wide berth to."

Now he really didn't like where this conversation headed. He accepted no praise from her compliment. "I don't want to control you, Harley."

"My real name is Hailey. Cute, huh? Hailey-Harley. At the time, Mary Jo and I thought we were so clever."

"Is that what you want me to call you?" He waited while she mulled his question over, hoping she'd answer "no." As much as he wanted to learn everything he could about this woman, he already loved the part of her that would forever remain "Harley." At least, to him.

"You can call me whatever you like. They're both me."

"I sure as hell hope so." His tone contained more force than he'd planned and he witnessed her subtle flinch. He concentrated on softening his voice before he spoke again. "Listen to me, Harley. I'm not Paul. I'm not your aunt. I want to love you, not control you."

Again, she combed her hands through her hair roughly. "Don't you see, you already control me!" Her voice crackled with despair. "From the moment I woke up in your arms, I've depended on you to take care of me. Hell, I insisted on it. I haven't made a single move without considering how it would affect you and your career."

"That only shows how selfless you are."

"I don't want to be selfless, Grant. I want to be self-ish. Make my own way. Put my needs first. I've never done that."

Grant stood, and stepped back, fighting the urge to grab her by the shoulders and shake some sense into her. "And what about Sammy?"

"That's different. He's a kid. He needs me."

"Then leaving me won't make a difference. You'll still be putting someone else's needs above your own." He leaned down, allowing himself to touch her hand. He bit back a growl when she stiffened. "Stay with me. You and Sammy are more than welcome here. Mary Jo, too, if she needs a place."

"I'm sure Mr. Phipps would have a field day with that scenario."

"I don't give a damn about him. Just you. Only you."

"Lord, Grant. Don't you see? You're willing to put me first over everything in your life. Your family. Your career. I can't do that. I may have my memory back, but I still don't know who I am. What I'm made of. Until I do…"

He held his hand up, cutting her off, silencing her painful truths. As much as he wanted to fight her, her reasoning remained firmly rooted. He wouldn't change her mind.

Not today anyway.

From the corner of his eye, he watched her swipe moisture from her face. "I don't know how to repay you for all you've done, for all you've risked."

His bittersweet smile felt foreign on his face. He stood, straightened his trousers, then glanced around at the meaningless representations of wealth and power all around him. His Mercedes and his Explorer gleamed from the street. His mansion loomed behind him. The entire Citrus Hill police force scrambled carefully over his lawn to ensure quick and certain justice for the man who probably directed at least some portion of their personal assets.

And still, he had nothing of value so long as Harley wouldn't have him in her life.

"You don't have to repay anything. Not now. You get your life how you want it, then look me up." He spared her a sidelong glance, then turned his back to make sure she didn't see the pain in his eyes. "We'll discuss reimbursement then."

13

GRANT STUFFED THE wrinkled napkin into the pocket of his slacks. The address scribbled in Mary Jo's hurried hand matched the numbers on the converted warehouse, leaving no doubt that the brass key would unlock the building's private side entrance. In a matter of minutes, he could end the nearly month-long separation Harley had imposed after leaving his home in Citrus Hill. Allowing her to maintain her privacy hadn't been easy, but he'd reverted to throwing himself into his work.

But when Mary Jo stopped by his office this afternoon on her way to pick up Sammy in Miami, he coerced her into allowing him to take her to lunch. She skillfully avoided telling him too much about how Harley was, saying he should find out for himself. Only gentle badgering and a strong dose of charm garnered a report that Harley had reclaimed her studio lease and had successfully started her therapy practice, thanks in part to the publicity generated by Mrs. Langley's newspaper articles.

Both Harley and Mary Jo had been careful to keep Grant's name out of reports regarding Buck's attack and subsequent arrest. With the long list of felony charges pending against Mary Jo's ex-boyfriend, Harley's assault complaint was hardly news of note for the big city papers. But the truest test came a week after Harley's departure, when Wilhelmina Langley's exposé dominated the front-page section of the *Citrus Hill Weekly*.

He'd received an advance copy, left mysteriously on his doorstep the night before. In words Grant found surprisingly poetic, Mrs. Langley told Harley's tale with compelling clarity and compassion. His neighbor slanted the piece into the story of a woman's quest for independence—and made the article a three-part essay that had concluded just the Sunday before. Buoyed by Mary Jo and Joy's more tragic stories, Harley came across as the most fortunate. She'd at least found a benevolent knight in shining armor in the financial impresario who risked his standing in a conservative community to help her rediscover her path.

The Board of Directors couldn't have been more pleased. Their CEO was a regular hero. The percentage of female investors surged—especially among those who'd previously left in protest over the libidinous activities of the former management. Howell Phipps protested the Board's dismissive attitude, and suffered a forced early retirement as a result. A unanimous vote promoted Grant to Chairman and CEO before he knew what was happening.

But Grant didn't give a damn about the good press, the firm's growth or his new position. He only wanted Harley back.

And now, after nearly a month of isolation, Harley wanted to see him. After she finished her burger and fries, Mary Jo slipped him the address and the key, told him to arrive at the studio at eight o'clock sharp, and left the restaurant.

Grant glanced at his watch. Seven fifty-two. Sunset neared, casting the old brick buildings with a magenta glow. Mingled sounds of pounding bass from the blues club two doors down and the Latin cantina across the street surged in the air, lending a breath of life to the red brick streets and cracked sidewalks. In the fifteen minutes since Grant arrived in Ybor City, Tampa's historic section nearly doubled in population. An hour more and the number would double again. Dressed in clothes ranging from power suits to spikes and leather, people of all ages swarmed the sidewalks. They pressed into Grant's personal space, urging him to open the door leading to Harley's second floor studio—or at least, move out of the way.

Now, he had to admit, if only to himself, how he both dreaded and anticipated this reunion. He replayed their last conversation at least ten times daily, feeling her conviction to make her own way—alone— like a knife in the heart. He'd read and reread Harley's interview with Mrs. Langley where she'd announced her commitment to complete autonomy from all outside influences. Now that she'd started down the road to her dream, how could she backtrack for him? How could he let her? More than likely, she planned tonight's rendezvous as a bittersweet, but definite goodbye.

Over his dead body.

Grant had the door unlocked then relocked in what seemed like a split second. He took the stairs three at a time, surprisingly unwinded when he burst through the entrance to her studio.

He didn't know what to expect in a dance therapist's studio, but he hadn't expected this.

With shades drawn, the polished wood floor caught and echoed the soft glow of violet-and-blue lights suspended from the ceiling. Sound equipment sat, silent, behind a mirrored privacy panel in one corner and large speakers dominated the other three. Four mirrored walls reflected his image and that of a simple wooden chair placed dead center in the room, directly across from a gleaming brass pole that stretched from the floor to the top of a sixteen-foot ceiling. A single red beam of light focused straight down on the seat.

In the muted darkness, he missed the spiral, wrought iron staircase at the far end of the room—until Harley emerged through the sliding door on the landing and called his name.

He took another step into the room, shutting the door behind him.

"Am I late?" he asked.

The metal landing rattled when Harley stepped closer to the edge. "If you are, it's my fault. I should have invited you long before now."

Grant blinked, wishing his eyes would adjust to the light so he could see her more clearly. Her silhouette hovered above him like a dark angel—mysterious, fascinating. Sad. Like someone about to say goodbye. "I understand."

"I don't think you do."

She pulled something from her pocket and a moment later the speakers awoke. The sensuous sound of a sultry saxophone masked the noise from the nightlife outside. The brass instrument wailed in perfect stereo, slowly, soulfully, a steady bass beat the only accompaniment. Then violins. Sweet. Innocent. Classic. The contrast of sound met and mingled with the lights and the mood. Grant closed his eyes and allowed the music to penetrate and dispel his reluctance and his fears, leaving nothing inside him but love and desire for Harley.

"Have a seat," she directed, though she made no move to descend to the studio's lower level.

Grant complied, not knowing what she had in mind. The red lamp heated the seat of the chair. Feeling warmer with each second that passed, Grant slid open the top button of his shirt and unknotted his tie.

"Comfortable?" Her voice, cast from a distance, reached his ear like an intimate whisper.

"I'm getting more and more uncomfortable by the minute."

He imagined that tiny, knowing smile of hers and his discomfort increased.

He heard her take a step down the staircase, but could barely see her with the bright red light beaming into his eyes. Scooting the chair forward an inch allowed him to break through the scarlet haze.

"That makes two of us."

She wore her trench coat, which she shed halfway down, folding it neatly over the handrail. He couldn't determine the exact style of her clothes beneath, but he prayed for something sexy, something she'd chosen just for him…something he'd rip off the moment she came close enough.

When she took a few more steps downward, he caught the distinct gloss of black leather.

His frustrated groan sounded distinctly like a feral growl.

"Harley, if you'd learned anything about me, you wouldn't be wearing that. Not unless you're prepared for the consequences."

She pulled the leather jacket's collar up stiffly. "I'm counting on those consequences, Mr. Riordan."

Spoken in the silkiest tone, her assertion quickened his pulse, diverting his blood flow exclusively to his lower body. His lungs tightened. His palms moistened. Her spiked heels clicked on the wood floor, a devilish cadence against the cool jazz on the stereo.

"Speaking of learning about people—" She remained just outside his line of sight. "I've found out a lot about myself in the last month."

She circled behind him. The spiced cinnamon scent she'd worn the first night they'd met teased his nostrils, spurring him to inhale despite the cramping in his chest.

"Like how sexy you are? How irresistible?"

"More like how stubborn."

Grant stifled a laugh, recalling that first night when she'd insisted on sleeping in his bed. And when she'd burst into his office. When she'd seduced him in the pool. "You're a woman who knows what she wants. There's no crime in that."

"There is when it stands in the way of love."

His heart skipped one beat, then a second when she stepped around him. Leaning seductively against the brass pole directly in front of him, but painfully out of his reach, she slid one foot up the sturdy shaft and balanced her spiked heel on the golden metal. Her leather pants hugged her calves and thighs like slick enamel.

"After regaining my memory, I couldn't see how I could get my life back on track if I stuck around your place. I thought I'd fall into my old habits, defer to you like I had to Aunt Gracie, and then to Paul, not make decisions for myself."

"Now you know differently?" Grant didn't want to let his hopes soar, but neither could he let this conversation draw out any longer than a few more minutes. Watching her stand there, her body undulating almost imperceptibly to the music, made him rock-hard. At the first confirmation that she wanted him back, he planned to divest her of her seductive clothes and make love to her right there on the chair.

Or against the pole.

Probably both.

Then, they'd move to the stairs. And beyond.

Her eyelashes fanned her cheeks as she glanced demurely downward. "Making decisions for myself has its merits, but it's lonely. Especially when I know there's someone out there who might want to share the process with me."

His throat constricted, momentarily abating his vivid fantasies.

"I spend all day dealing with people who aren't sure about what they want." He leaned forward on his elbows, the red light heating the back of his neck. "Who want my approval sometimes more than my advice. Who want me to make their choices so they don't have to blame themselves when they make a mistake. I tire of that responsibility. I want a woman who knows what she wants, but who needs me to make the getting more…enjoyable."

"I may need more than that sometimes."

"Sweetheart, you know I'll give you everything I have. Just don't make me wait any longer."

A half smile tugged at the corner of her lips, but she managed, visibly, to keep her grin at bay. Instead, she lowered her foot and balanced her weight, as if preparing for action.

"Isn't that chair hard?"

The curved wooden back did bite into his shoulders, but it was the ache troubling his groin he needed Harley to alleviate. "I'd much prefer a soft bed."

She pulled down the gleaming silver zipper on her jacket, exposing the pale bare skin of her throat. "You sure? The bedroom upstairs is tiny. Hardly enough room for what I have planned."

She spun around to the other side of the pole, undulating right and left as the music's tempo increased. "I couldn't strip for you that night by the pool. I kept thinking that I'd done that for other men."

Grant fought to take a swallow. "But you never have."

"Now, I want to." She turned around, leaning her back against the pole, sliding down a few inches so the thick gold post slipped between the crease of her buttocks. "For you."

Sitting back, Grant gripped the edge of the chair, hardly believing how Harley, the woman he loved— the woman he intended to marry—was about to play out his most secret fantasy. "You know what you want. Don't let me stand in your way."

She flipped the cropped jacket down her arms and coyly glanced over her bared shoulder. "I don't intend to let you stand. House rules. No touching the dancers."

He licked parched lips. "Not at all? Ever?"

The leather jacket hit the floor. Harley kicked it away.

"Not until I say so."

Facing him again, she stood, legs parted, so the pole fit into her cleavage. She reached both hands above her head, grasping the brass and swaying her hips—two counts right, three to the left. Slowly, she inched her hands downward, stroking the post sensually, leaving Grant to imagine how she'd touch him when the time came.

Leaning her head back, Harley surrendered to the music. The deliberate beat guided her hands as she released the pole and unzipped her pants. She dipped a finger into the crotch, teasingly, tantalizingly, showing Grant how she adored her body, how she wanted him to adore her body. Soon. Very soon.

Two quick tugs with her other hand and the Velcro

seams released. The pants flew across the room. In only a leather bikini and ankle-high boots, Harley grasped the pole again, spinning and jumping at the same time until she swung around with practiced grace.

She landed crouched close to the floor. Bracing the pole against her back, she stood, languidly, again positioning the brass between her legs, rolling her hips forward and back, simulating sex, feigning rapture on her face.

Sweat trickled down Grant's forehead and collected at his collar, but the heat didn't stop there. Every inch of him flamed with intense need. His breathing labored, he parted his lips, pulling in deep breaths, panting openly, and not caring. Without any prodding from him, she knew exactly what he craved. She plunged into the role of seductress with verve, invigorating herself with the power of her control, vitalizing him with the novelty of complete surrender.

She left the pole and stood not a half foot from where he sat. Starting at her neck, she smoothed her hands down the side of her body, rolling her hips in rhythmic circles. Thrusting forward, she bent her knees so her breasts bounced just inches from his lips.

She pulled at a snap on the top of the triangular bikini cup, revealing a sliver of skin on her right breast, then her left. Two more tugs, and the top would become nothing more than black straps surrounding pale, ample breasts.

Anticipation left him speechless.

"Enjoying the show?"

He managed to nod.

"You look hot."

Stepping between his legs, she removed his tie and tugged his shirt from his pants, working the buttons until the material fell aside.

"I want you comfortable."

She rubbed his shirt against her face and inhaled his scent before she tossed the garment aside.

"Then let me touch you."

"Not yet."

She undid his belt next, then the button and zipper of his pants. Her fingers momentarily brushed over his stiffness. He groaned.

She backed away. "Ever had a lap dance?"

"Ever done one?"

She grinned at his evasion, obviously confident the Grant Riordan she knew would never have the nerve to purchase something so forbidden in a public place.

"This'll be my first." With deft fingers, she removed the triangles of material covering her breasts. Her nipples, bathed in the red heated light, peaked high, announcing her arousal.

She turned around, braced her hands on her knees and crouched, balancing her backside a breath away from his lap.

"Marry me and it won't be your last," he promised.

She grinned wickedly over her shoulder, dipping to briefly allow contact between her bottom and his groin. "Intend to hire me out?"

He gripped the side of the chair tighter. "Not on your life. I'll keep you as my own private dancer."

Facing him, she climbed over his lap, not sitting and still moving to the music. Her eyes now misted with something deeper than seduction—something more akin to fearful hope.

"You really want to marry me?"

He saw the last vestiges of uncertainty in her eyes, and vowed to devote himself to proving how unwarranted her apprehension was. In all his life, he'd never met a woman who embodied the exact combination of intelligence, sensuality and daring he craved. He was helpless to resist her, powerless to let her go. He grasped her waist, pulling her full against him, showing her how much he needed her at that moment while he told her how he needed her for the rest of his life.

"Right now, I want to make love to you. But tomorrow I want to marry you. This last month's been hell. It's been my old life. You're the key to my new life. I love you, Harley. Be my wife. Be my lover and my confidant. My partner."

"Your private dancer?"

Just weeks ago, the idea that she removed her clothes for a man's pleasure terrified her—even when the man was Grant. But since she'd left his house, she'd learned how deeply he'd imbued himself into her soul. How the mere thought of him set her mind racing with delicious decadence and her heart with rapid need. She'd fully recovered her memory, but still couldn't believe a time existed when Grant wasn't a crucial part of her. Seducing Grant back into her life had been her way to promise she'd never let his life get boring or predictable ever again.

Amid her fears that he'd sap her independence, she'd missed how his presence fortified her, how his desire emboldened her. Even beyond the bedroom, their love gave her an equilibrium she'd never known. And once she dropped all pretense of humility, she realized she provided the same symmetry to him.

They were opposite sides of a scale. Their love would keep them in perfect balance.

He grinned as he leaned forward and took a nipple between his lips. "Yeah, my private dancer."

She moaned, then cooed when he suckled gently. "On one condition."

Looking up from where he now laved between her

breasts, Grant's eyes promised her the world. "Name your price."

She divested him of his pants, then unsnapped the side of her bikini bottoms and slid the material away.

Naked and unbound, Grant grasped her hips, posing her directly over him. His eyes reflected such intense love, she feared speaking and breaking the spell.

But she had to ask this. She had to know that she'd never lose the man fate gave her and the ecstasy his loving promised.

"Don't ever let me forget how much I love you."

Grant slipped his hand between her legs. In a split second, a warm, slick heat pooled and bubbled. He eased her down, entering her with such exquisite laziness, she knew she'd climax before the first thrust.

"Harley, honey, I'm going to love you so thoroughly, tonight, tomorrow, and every day after, you'll forget everything but me. Think you can handle that?"

She could only murmur her consent before the room began to spin.

If you enjoyed what you just read,
then we've got an offer you can't resist!

Take 2 bestselling love stories FREE!

Plus get a FREE surprise gift!

Temptation®

COMING NEXT MONTH

#725 JUST FOR THE NIGHT Leandra Logan
Bachelor Auction

Shari Johnson had spent her *entire* inheritance bidding on Garrett McNamara! Secretly she fantasized about the gorgeous bachelor and wanted him "just for the night." No strings. After all, she ran a coffee shop...and he was a millionaire. But Shari hadn't counted on him wanting her every night—forever.

#726 SAY "AHHH..." Donna Sterling
Bedside Manners, Book 1

Dr. Connor Wade thought he had a pretty good bedside manner...until his newest patient, Sarah Flowers, almost ran from his office at the mere sight of him. But Sarah had her reasons. She'd been expecting old Doc Bronkowski, and no way was she going to bare her soul—or anything else—to Dr. Tall Dark 'n' Handsome!

#727 TANGLED SHEETS Jo Leigh
The Wrong Bed

Maggie Beaumont was determined to seduce her fiancé, Gary, at the masquerade party. But somehow in the dark she ended up in the arms of the *wrong* man! Or was Spencer really Mr. Right? He was sexy, loving—and determined to have Maggie to himself.

#728 BREATHLESS Kimberly Raye
Blaze

Ten years ago, Tack Brandon hightailed it out of Inspiration, Texas, leaving behind his home, his family—and the girl he'd made a woman. Now he's back—and Annie Divine wants to get even. Following Tack's example, she planned to love him within an inch of his life...and then walk away. If only his kisses didn't leave her breathless....